WRAITH

The New Mythology
Book 3

MATT KING

Wraith

Copyright © 2025 Matt King

All rights reserved.

No part of this book may be reproduced, distributed, or transmitted in any form or by any means, including photocopying, recording, or other electronic or mechanical methods, without the prior written permission of the publisher, except in the case of brief quotations embodied in critical reviews and certain other noncommercial uses permitted by copyright law. For permission requests, contact the publisher at contactus@bdapublishing.c0m.

This is a work of fiction. Names, characters, places, and incidents are either the product of the author's imagination or used fictitiously. Any resemblance to actual persons, living or dead, events, or locales is entirely coincidental.

Published by BDA Publishing

86 Victory Lane, Boyce, Virginia 22620

https://bdapublishing.com

eBook ISBN: 978-1-965743-00-3

Physical ISBN: TBA

Library of Congress Control Number (LCCN): TBA

Cover Design: TBA

Editing: TBA

First edition: May 2025

Printed in the United States of America.

Wraith | Matt King

*For anyone who has suffered pain
carried out in the name of love.*

Introduction

A Note About My Connected Universe

THE CIRCLE WAR books kicked off a series of events that laid the foundation for a new era of heroes and myths—what I call THE NEW MYTHOLOGY. Millions of years later, Prism and Atalanta were the first of those heroes.

One of the casualties of the Circle War was, of course, Earth. It took a lot to rebuild this planet, and even though August left behind blueprints on how to restore our society, not everything is an exact copy. You'll notice some difference in the terms people use (year 21, for instance, instead of 21 years old) and countries are non-existent, replaced by city-states under the guidance of the World Union. It might seem like a lot to decipher, but you'll get the hang of it. I have faith in you.

So, do you need to read the Circle War books to know what's going on? Absolutely not. Should you anyway? Maybe if you love easter eggs because they're all over the place here.

I really hope you enjoy this new entry in the New Mythology series. I'm so excited to go back to this world, and

Wraith's story will add a whole new (semi-terrifying) dimension. Whether **WRAITH** is your first book in this universe or the sixth, I appreciate you being here.

CHAPTER ONE

VALHALLA TOWER STOOD like a sword between the Pacific Ocean and Seattle's Cascade Mountains. There was a sense of protection about the ebony monolith that settled my overworked nerves, but it was also daunting and unfamiliar. I reminded myself I'd come to Seattle to reclaim the person I used to be, and that the old Zoe Daniel would've been excited to find a place like Valhalla where she could bury herself in a new research project. She would've relished the challenge. I put on a smile to pretend to be her again.

Stepping into the lobby was the first test of my temporary veneer. I'd gone all morning without thinking about Britt; but as I walked through the revolving doors, a woman passed by that could have been her twin. Long brown hair wrapped in a braid, athletic frame, sharp features. Her eyes were even green. My breathing shallowed.

She's a thousand miles behind me, I told myself.

I'd made sure there could be no breadcrumbs for her to follow—applying for jobs on library computers, stashing away clothes for months, claiming the laundry service kept losing our clothes so she wouldn't suspect I was packing my things. I even had my old job put away a small percentage of my check each week, telling Britt I'd started a fund to send her back to school. The fact that I survived to walk through the doors of Valhalla Tower surely meant my idea had worked. But even now, three days later, I couldn't shake the feeling she'd figure out my plan and take me back to La Grange. She'd never let me have this. I'd die in a city where no one cared about me except her—the last in a series of Britt's isolations.

The sounds of the lobby swelled. At once, I could hear every voice, every minute noise as though it was a blaring alarm bell rattling through my ears.

I quickly reached for my earbuds. *She's not here. She can't find me.*

Even wearing my noise-canceling earbuds, the sounds of the busy lobby still bled through, but the volume was manageable now. My misophonia was always worse when I was nervous. Chewing, sniffling, pouring drinks over ice, the high-pitched whine of console screens—sounds most people ignored, but when my stress was high, they were like pouring iodine over a paper cut. The earbuds at least gave me a fighting chance on bad days.

Come on, Zoe. You've got a job offer to negotiate.

A bank of elevators took up most of the wall on the right side of the lobby. There were doors marked for the first thirty-nine floors, and others for floors forty-one to fifty but not to the fortieth. In the middle of the bank was another elevator door, unmarked with no call button and only a small metal plate on the wall beside it. I re-checked the email on my phone. The last direction was to take the elevator from the lobby to the fortieth floor.

I took out one of my earbuds and walked to the main desk situated beneath an angular set of stairs leading to a mezzanine. A man looked up at me with a well-rehearsed smile. He was easily year sixty-five despite the jet-black hair and beaming white dentures.

"How can I help you, dearest?" He had the voice of someone who took smoke breaks seriously.

"I'm trying to get to a job interview."

The smell of cologne hit me in a delayed shockwave as he stood to take out a well-worn map of the building's floors. The edges were frayed, like he'd had it since the building opened.

"I don't suppose you know the name of the person you're looking for?" he asked.

I paused, giving myself enough time to swallow the smartass answer that almost came out. "It's Gemma Weeks. The invite just said to meet on the fortieth floor."

"Ah. You're going to Research. Well then, head back to those elevators," he said, pointing. He folded his map along well-worn creases. "Middle door. Just put your palm on the reader, and you'll be on your way."

That couldn't be right. "Are you sure? I don't remember sending them any biotelemetry data for the scan."

The man smirked and sank back in his rolling chair. "Welcome to Valhalla."

I re-inserted my earbud, trying my best to push down the rising tide of suspicion. They work with the World Union— that's why they have my data. No need to search the shadows for monsters.

The unmarked elevator opened as soon as I put my palm on the cool metal plate. The inside of the car had a penetrating chemical smell, like they were using Feristrol as an air freshener. The scent was familiar, almost homey. Most of the labs I'd worked in smelled the same way after the overnight cleaning crews finished. It made my breakfast coffee taste like a bleach latte.

The elevator doors stayed closed for a beat at the end of the ride, as if they wanted to make my entrance more dramatic. I used the time to take my earbuds out and hide them in my shoulder bag. Once the doors parted, a busy office greeted me with a view all the way to the other side of the floor. I got tired just thinking about walking that far to get to my desk each morning. There was no admin to check in with, only an empty chair with a "Be back soon" sign, followed by rows upon rows of cubicles with white half-walls and little glass dividers along shared borders. Scattered around the maze were rolling tables with coffee carafes and baskets of snacks. The only part of the floor plan that wasn't open was a large walled-off section dominating the back right quadrant of the office, accessed through a single door with the word **BIOLABS** stenciled on it. It looked like one of those *Coming Soon* sections in airports where generic white panels hid the construction going on behind the scenes.

"Zoe?"

I turned to see a middle-aged woman striding confidently toward me, loose red curls bobbing up and down like springs. It reminded me of the time I tried to impress one of the boys in my college chemistry lab and ended up making my hair look like a bowl of pasta. Hers were done perfectly, though. The flowers on her dress even matched the shade of her hair. She had a mother's smile—it was the only way to describe it. Some women just looked like they could take any stray and raise them to be President.

I liked her right away.

"I'm Gemma Weeks," she said, shaking my hand. "It's good to finally meet you after so much back and forth. Did you find the place okay?"

I laughed. "This building is hard to miss. I saw it as soon as I drove over the mountains."

"Right? It's ridiculous. Somebody graduated architecture school with a little too much to prove if you ask me. Come on. I'll show you to the labs."

I pined for my earbuds as I walked behind her. The office was a buzz of noise, mumbled conversations mixed with the clacking of keyboards and pens rapping on desktops. It didn't help that I was starting to get nervous about negotiations again. Nerves only turned up the volume in my head.

Everyone we passed either waved or tried to flag Gemma down for a conversation. "Ms. Weeks, can I borrow you real quick?" a guy asked, jogging over to us.

"Not now, Abner. Visit you after?"

Visit. I half-wondered if she'd bring cookies.

"Your lab space certainly stands out," I told her. It was the best small talk I could make about a huge box taking up a quarter of the office.

"It's mostly for the benefit of the people out here in the cubes. For someone in Marketing or Government Relations, it can be tough to look at what we do and get really excited about what they're representing. It's human nature to want to impress others, though, so I made this part of the company look mysterious and important. In turn, they feel important by being associated with it. Make sense?"

"I think so." I wouldn't have guessed so much thought went into a set of white walls.

It took two swipes of separate security cards before we were allowed through to the Biolabs door. Once inside, she let out a sigh and gestured down the hall. "I love my non-research colleagues, but this is the only place I can relax. Come on, we're just down here."

She led us to a small conference room with a presentation console screen on the wall. I wanted to touch it. Those kinds of interactive screens cost more money than I'd ever made in a month. Gemma took the closest chair and offered me the one beside her. It was the first time I'd noticed that she didn't have anything with her—not a handheld or even a slip of paper with my resume on it. Under any other circumstances, I'd assume she was calling me in to tell me I didn't get the job.

"So, you're from La Grange," she said. "That's a hike from here. What drew you to Seattle?"

It was probably the only thing I'd answer quickly all day,

the result of endless hours in the rental car rehearsing my excuse. "The heat," I said, suddenly realizing that I'd memorized the answer to why I left, not what tempted me to come. I stammered. "I mean, it's hot back in La Grange. Not here. Here is nice."

"Yes, it is."

"Have you been?" I asked, trying to buy time for my brain to cool down from panic mode. "To La Grange, I mean. I know you've been here."

Oh my gods, just walk out now, Zoe. Save yourself.

"I dated a guy from there once," she replied. "Small...*guy* energy, if you know what I mean."

She laughed and I joined in. "That checks out."

With the ice broken, I no longer felt like a prized pig trying for a blue ribbon. I set my bag on the floor and pulled out my resume along with a few published articles.

"Oh, you don't need that," she said. "I think I know all there is to know about you."

I wondered how that could be true. I felt an initial tinge of fear at the thought of someone researching my past instead of hearing the curated story I'd made for them. I had to remind myself that this kind of background check was probably done by every company I'd ever worked for—they just didn't admit it. She was only doing her job.

"You've had quite the career so far, Zoe. Microcellular research is a tough field to advance in. Really impressive."

"Thank you. I love what I do."

"But you don't spend too much time in one place doing it, do you?"

And just like that, I was off my script again. I panicked at the thought of having to discuss Britt's nomadic moves as an effort to keep me isolated and the pressure I felt to stay with her. I lowered my head.

"Testing the waters, I imagine," Gemma said, filling in the

answer for me. Her expression shifted some, like she felt the sudden tension and looked to provide a release.

"You know how people out of school are," I said. "No one settles down for the first few years."

"Are you saying you're past that?"

She was direct without seeming judgmental. I admired that. I wasn't totally unprepared for the question, though, and straightened up to answer. "Where I live isn't as important to me as the work I do, and I've been really impressed with what I've seen from Valhalla, especially your work with targeted cellular treatment. It seems like there's no shortage of professional challenges."

It was the answer she wanted to hear. I could tell by the brightness returning to her eyes. "It is pretty exciting here," she said. "I can only say so much until you sign on, but…it's beyond cutting edge. I don't think you'll find another place like it."

I decided to go ahead with one of the questions everyone had been dodging so far in my interview process. "How does my research background fit in with the project you have for me?"

Gemma sat back with a wry smile. "Clever time to ask that question. You waited until I was gushing about work. Smart. But, you'll have to hold on a bit longer. What I can tell you is that it's probably the most impactful work you'll ever do."

I felt like a child shaking a present to figure out what was inside, and Gemma was the mother enjoying the struggle.

She waved her hand across the top of the meeting room table and a console beneath the glass came to life. She tapped a few commands to start a screencast on the wall behind me. "HR says I have to show you this *very important* video about the company culture," she said, her eyes focused on finding the file she was looking for. "Let's get this commercial out of the way, and then we'll go for a walk."

She wasn't kidding about it being a commercial. The

video was full of cheery people working in labs, bookkeeping, sales—just about any position you could think of at the company—and they were all thrilled to the point of permanent smiles. It reminded me of the videos I used to watch in my mom's travel agency as a kid, each one promising an idyllic escape from the doldrums of life. Something about the look on the actors' faces always made me sad. They had to pretend that life could be so good.

Gemma checked her phone while it played. Eventually it got to the story that drew me to Valhalla. It mentioned several areas of emerging research Valhalla spearheaded that were right in my wheelhouse—including microcellular studies. There were only a handful of tech firms in America that could say that. Most of the advanced work was done in the Triton office of the World Union. I couldn't bring myself to sign up for a government job, no matter how much they recruited me. I needed to make a living wage.

Somewhat disjointedly, the HR hard sell switched to an empty red screen. The closer I looked, the more I saw that it wasn't really empty. The sea of red was moving subtly, like something stirred beneath the surface. It eventually faded to black, replaced by a title placard—*Out of Chaos, Renewal.*

"That was my addition," Gemma whispered proudly.

I smiled through the disconcerting effect the red, writhing screen left behind.

After a painfully composed jingle closed the video, she shut the presentation down. "Now for the good stuff. You can leave your things here."

She motioned for me to follow. After going down a few nondescript hallways, we walked into the heart of the lab.

I used to dream of places like this. There were multiple electron microscopes and enough clean labs for a dozen researchers. I loved clean labs. I did my best work when I had the room to myself, and clean labs were only meant for one. As we walked, I counted four walk-in refrigeration chambers along with modeling quantum consoles and comfort-first office chairs that probably cost more than my first car.

It was like Winter's Day for lab nerds. I wanted to start work on the spot.

I think I'm home.

"I envy how you must be feeling," Gemma said. "I don't get to do much actual research anymore now that I'm in management. Places like this used to make me giddy."

"It's impressive," I replied, trying to temper my enthusiasm. "What would my responsibilities be? I mean, if we can come to an agreement."

Gemma smiled. "*If* you decide to work here, you'd be a Senior Researcher reporting directly to me. I'd put you right over there." She pointed to a corner of the lab with an electron microscope, quantum console, L-shaped desk, and attached clean lab. We stopped at the entrance to another researcher's station. The woman acknowledged us with a polite smile in between switching slides. Her modeling console showed a strand of DNA on its screen.

"Can I be honest for a moment?" Gemma said.

I nodded. "Of course."

"I've been following your career for a while now. Not in a stalkery way, of course, but in more of a...*fan* way, let's say. Someone passed me one of your grad school papers a couple of years ago. It read like something I would've written when I was your age. I tried to contact you back then for a job offer but your adviser never passed along the meeting request, I gather."

I shook my head. "That sounds about right. She always wanted me to work for the World Union."

Gemma rolled her eyes. "Sheep."

Exactly. Other than not being able to afford groceries, it was the main reason I stayed away from anything linked to the WU. They told you what to study rather than letting you find the path that interested you most.

"Listen," Gemma said. "Not to be too informal, but I feel like I can sense when things are a good fit, and you and I would work well together here. I like to get out of people's way, and you seem happiest when you're heads-down in the work. Is that fair to say?"

"It is."

"Thought so. It's settled then. If HR asks, just tell them I went through a lot of back and forth before offering you a max contract. We really want you here, Zoe. *I* want you here. You can work on a year-to-year contract, too. Whatever you feel is best."

Max contract? I could hardly believe it. Research salaries were heavily regulated to keep company competition fair. A max contract was like being handed a lottery ticket. I could already envision the two—no, three—bedroom place I'd be able to afford.

"What do you say?"

There was no reason to be coy. I was home and I knew it. And yet, I couldn't help the small seed of doubt that wanted to take root in my mind. How could anything really be this perfect?

Britt will find a way to ruin this. She'll make me wish I'd never crossed her.

"Thinking about the possibilities?" Gemma asked.

I blinked my way out of my mini-nightmare and dug in my heels, unwilling to fall down the same familiar slope into the shadow of Britt. "Just trying to sort everything out. Of course, I'd love to work here if you'll have me."

Gemma clapped her hands together. She looked like she wanted to give me a hug, and I was so happy to finally be in a current of optimism, I might've accepted it.

"Take the night to get things in order, Zoe. I'm sure you have lots to arrange. Do you have a place picked out yet?"

Other than the hotel room, I hadn't. I didn't want to risk it without a contract. "I was reading online about some apartments on the other side of the bay that sounded nice."

Gemma scoffed. "Trust me, you don't want those. Taking the ferry every morning seems like a good idea until you're stuck sitting beside a mid-level banker shouting on their cell phone. Why not look at the South Street district?"

South Street was a popular new residential district just south of downtown. It was a dream spot. It was also completely out of my price range.

Not with a max contract, it isn't.

"Do you have anywhere specific I could look?" I asked, dipping my toes in the unfamiliar waters of financial security.

"Try Havenwood Village. Valhalla has an arrangement with them that would speed things along. Plus, I know the owner, and I'll make sure they let you stay for free while you're working out details."

"Oh no, I couldn't do that. It's too much. I don't mind looking around."

Gemma waved her hand. "Nonsense. It's a new development, and the apartments are nicely put together. Plus, it's close to my favorite noodle place. If you're looking for a spot to celebrate all the money I'm about to pay you, Malay's is it."

I didn't even mind the obvious fishing attempt for gratitude. "Thank you. Really, this is all a dream come true."

"I'm so excited," she said. "We'll get you going straight away. Just head back up here tomorrow morning, and you can sign your non-disclosures. After that, I can finally tell you what you'll be working on. Just wait until you see what the Chaos Project holds."

Chaos. The name made me uncomfortable. I'd had enough chaos in my life already. Valhalla promised renewal out of chaos, though. I could only hope.

After a few more paperwork formalities, I left the office in a daze, not quite sure whether my whirlwind romance with Gemma and Valhalla was real or not. Gemma gave me the employee manual to take home to read, as well as a few bios on the people I'd be working with. It was the only thing keeping me from assuming the whole interview had been a figment of my imagination. I put in my earbuds and scanned the papers while I walked. The white noise helped me concentrate on the legalese.

Havenwood was only six blocks from the Valhalla Tower doors. I stood at the entry with my fingers hovering over the handle, unable to make myself go inside. For every good thing suddenly happening to me, there were a dozen past bruises competing to drown out my hope—I couldn't survive on my own…I couldn't live up to the promise of my past work…I couldn't escape Britt.

A woman about my age wandered out the other door and gave me a strange look before getting in a mag-lev transit parked outside. I must have looked like an idiot standing there.

Come on, Zoe. You can't be afraid forever.

Britt would always be a threat, but she wasn't here, and I could hide myself in a city-state of millions. I had a job and a real future—a chance to be Zoe Daniel again.

I took out my earbuds and gripped the handle.

"Welcome home," the lobby clerk said as I walked inside.

"Thanks. It's good to finally be here."

CHAPTER TWO

I LEFT Havenwood the next morning with coffee in hand and a head full of thoughts about my first day working with Chaos. Companies always hype up a new project when they want to hire you, but Gemma made Chaos seem different, although I couldn't put a finger on why. Maybe it was the look that came over her when she started talking about the work. It was the kind of excitement you couldn't fake, and it was contagious. As I joined the flow of people walking downtown, all I could think about were possibilities. What would it be like to study something that wasn't already scrutinized to death? What was left to discover that could make a former lab rat like Gemma so excited?

Two sips of coffee later and I was already rehearsing my speech for the Orsix Foundation prize.

The new phone I'd bought after leaving Britt rang unexpectedly, interrupting my daydreams. I had to read the caller ID twice to make sure I wasn't hallucinating.

What in seven hells do these people want?

The screen told me it was a World Union office calling. Government clearance forms required a contact number, and the GC was one of a million online forms I'd filled out when I applied for the Valhalla job. Still, I hadn't expected them to call. Maybe Chaos was a bigger deal than I realized.

I took out an earbud to answer. "This is Zoe."

There was no response. I stopped walking and covered my other ear to drown out the sounds of the city. "Hello?"

A rustling sound came over the speaker, like someone moving their hand over the mic. I could hear them breathing.

My chest turned cold. "Britt?"

The line cut.

I stared at the screen, trying to figure out how she could've found my number. I'd been so careful. All around me, the volume of background noises started to swell. Car brakes scraped against metal. A thousand overlapping conversations needled at my ears. I jabbed my earbud back in, closed my eyes, and focused on the white noise coming through the speakers until I could get my breathing under control.

She can't find you. You covered your tracks. You left no trace.

I opened my eyes again to the tear-blurred sight of South Street. Eventually, I convinced my racing mind it was most likely a wrong number. Someone at the WU must have messed up and called by accident. People in the government made butt dials, too, right? Or maybe they just couldn't hear me.

One breath at a time, reason began to replace panic.

I had to forgive myself these types of reactions. There would always be a part of me that couldn't help looking over my shoulder for Britt. I might've left her behind, but that didn't mean she was gone.

Walking into the Valhalla lobby calmed some of the residual nerves left over from the phone call—which politely made room for all new worries. I couldn't help the growing fear that this new lease on life was going to be short-lived. The cushy job, the new apartment…it was all too perfect. Something had to give. That's just how the universe worked.

Thankfully, Gemma was waiting for me when I got off at the fortieth floor. She greeted me in a dark blue dress with matching heels. I didn't know why I was so fixated on her clothes. Nerves apparently made me a fashion reporter. A man that looked like he'd barely hit year twenty-one followed close behind, carrying a stack of folders and papers. His shirt was wrinkled in front.

"Zoe," Gemma said, beaming. "Welcome back! I'm so excited for you to be here. How was Havenwood?"

"Everything you said it'd be. I love it."

"Ah, to be single and in my twenties again. I'd live there in a minute." She paused for wistful effect. "Oh, before I forget, this is my Office Manager, Anjo. I wanted to get your HR paperwork out of the way quickly so we could get to the good stuff. Got your signing hand all loosened up?"

I wiggled my fingers.

"Good. Anjo here will step you through all the legal nonsense."

He tapped the top of his pile. "It's required—"

"And then I'll meet you in the lab," she said, looking at me as she patted him on the shoulder. The excitement in her voice still felt real. It was the tell-tale sign of a discovery addict —the thrill of new breakthroughs and new problems to solve. It made me wonder why she ever gave it up to be a manager.

Gemma walked down the rows of desks toward the labs, leaving me with Anjo and his stack of requirements.

"We can use the conference suite," he said, pointing to a room with a long meeting table surrounded by glass walls and a view of the Cascades.

The NDAs took almost a full hour to read through. I'd seen overly protective legal docs before, but nothing as paranoid as Valhalla's exclusivity pledges. Seemed weird that I had to promise never to give a TV interview without prior authorization from the Board, as if researchers ever made the news. Even Anjo seemed embarrassed by it, accepting each signed section like a greeter at a mortuary.

With the paperwork done, Anjo handed me a key card to

get me through to the labs. I wandered down the halls until I found Gemma waiting in a narrow break room, scrolling on her phone. For the first time since I'd met her, she wore a frown. When she saw me come in, she wiped it away and hastily replaced it with a smile.

"Ready to get started, I hope?"

"Beyond," I replied.

"Good. It's been killing me to keep this project a secret from you. If anyone can appreciate what we've found, it's the woman who made her name in reverse-engineering liposomes. Come on. I'll show you to your *other* new home."

Her mood seemingly replenished, I followed with a bounce in my own step as she led me through the halls I'd visited the day before. One set of glass dividers gave way to another, each cube filled by researchers busy looping through model structures or glued to a microscope. I paused at the office Gemma had pointed to as being mine during our tour, but she kept going, making me wonder if the bait-and-switch was on and I was about to be introduced to my new lab partners—bucket and pail.

It wasn't long until we got to an uninterrupted length of blank wall, which stood out in the densely packed open lab space.

"Place your hand over here." Gemma motioned to an empty spot in front of her. "Let's make sure your access works."

Curious, I hovered my palm over the bare section of wall, halfway wondering if this was some sort of first-day prank. A faint green glow from beneath the white surface appeared in an outline around my hand. Somewhere underneath, a hidden latch retracted as the door slid sideways into the wall, revealing a dimly lit lab. Split evenly by a plexiglass divider, one side was a spacious clean room with a single table inside protected by a sealed door, while the other contained a bank of consoles with LED keyboards projected on the tabletop. I'd only seen tech like that in articles.

Gemma looked between the consoles and me with a giddy smile. "Aren't they gorgeous?"

"They are. Are they zero-contaminant?"

She nodded. "I convinced the board we had to have them to deal with the unknowns of Chaos."

Clean rooms usually required a protective suit to go in and out. If anything got on the suit, like a virus or a bacterial sample, it might adhere to something like the surface of a physical keyboard, and nobody wanted to be responsible for starting the next plague. The brushed titanium console desk wouldn't allow for that kind of contamination, though, and with LED keyboards installed, I could type on the metal and it would read my strokes as if I were pressing actual keys. I hadn't been this excited to get my hands on something since that time my dad got me my first electric bike, and that thing had a bell I could program to play a siren when I passed people.

"Take a seat," Gemma said. "Let's get you going."

The metal-backed chair was surprisingly comfortable. The cushion was a non-porous bladder of silicone.

Gemma reached over to trace some gestures on the LED pad beside the keys. "You'll need to memorize that pattern," she said absently. The unlocked keyboard glowed to life. "And now, I want to introduce you to the first great discovery since the ancients created the Manhattan Project. Zoe, meet Chaos."

A whirring noise interrupted the stillness of the room behind the safety glass as a hole in the ceiling opened above the table. I could hardly stand still while I waited for the entrance. A glass cylinder no bigger than my arm descended through the opening, giving me my first glimpse of Chaos.

The substance was *alive*. It moved in ribbons along the inside of the glass tube like storms on the face of Jupiter, each rotating band a slightly different shade of deep red. I couldn't tell if I was looking at a liquid or a gas. It was opaque and looked like it had a surface, but something about its movements suggested it was as frictionless as air. Whatever it was, it sure as hell looked like it had the potential to be chaotic.

I wanted to start solving its riddle immediately.

"TS-2591, or as I call it—Chaos," Gemma said. "Valhalla has given the world so much, programmable T-cells and emergent virus predictive analysis, but all of it pales in comparison to the potential of that little red tube. It's going to make everyone in this building obscenely rich. I don't believe in magic, Zoe, but I can tell you this—I'm not sure I could ever explain the things we've seen this substance do. It's a godsend."

I was skeptical right away. Even the best magic could be explained. "Is there a special process to produce it? What kind of atomic structure does it have?"

She smiled at me over her shoulder as she opened a drawer under the desk to pull out a plain manila folder. "Here," she said, separating out a few pages. "I had Records declassify these for you. Take a look."

Paper reports were archaic, but not uncommon with high-security labs. I scanned the first sheet. It was a spectrometer reading showing the concentration percentages of elements. Even the simplest compounds had a mix of ingredients. This graph was blank.

"There must be something wrong with the instrument. It has to be made of something."

"Exactly what I said, so I had these tests run on three different machines."

She handed the entire folder to me, and I thumbed through the remaining pages, each one stating unequivocally that there were no known elements in the Chaos compound.

My mind raced. "This is unbelievable. It must be an

element no one has discovered before. A new inert gas, maybe? Or—"

Gemma shook her head. "Look closer."

I didn't know what good it would do to look through a bunch of blank results again, but I humored her. On the second-to-last page of the report, I saw what she alluded to.

"No. That can't be. That's impossible."

"Not impossible, Zoe."

What I'd missed the first time was the electron microscope scan. I hadn't given it a second thought because the page was blank like all the others, but when I thought about it again I realized it *couldn't* be blank. The scan was essentially a picture of the smallest molecules of a substance, a window into the connections that made elements like hydrogen and oxygen form water. The picture of Chaos showed nothing. It was like a vampire looking into a mirror.

I was in the same room with potentially the greatest scientific discovery our species had ever known. Finding a substance that defied everything we knew about biology and chemistry was like discovering a second Earth behind the sun. It turned everything on its head. I looked at the tube of Chaos again. It moved through the container like a hungry lion pacing behind a cage. At once, I was afraid to be anywhere near it, not because it scared me, but because of the enormity of it all. *Gemma's made a mistake*, I thought. *There should be a dozen top scientists studying this substance, not just me.*

"What's going through your head?" Gemma asked.

I wasn't sure what to list first. I decided on the obvious. "That this is beyond one person's research capabilities. That I'm not sure how to even approach it. That I'll waste what little we have."

"To start, don't think of it as a finite fragile object. One of the most unbelievable properties of Chaos is that it's self-replicating. If you ruin a sample, it'll just make more."

"Self-replicating?"

"Mmhmm." Gemma took the other seat and pulled it close to me. "That's not all. Chaos has the ability to *interface* with human bodies, for lack of a better term, just not in a repeatable pattern."

"What do you mean?"

She closed the folder and placed it on the desk. "I should tell you how it started first. You're aware of the World Union's push to study The Last Winter?"

"I think so. They're trying to confirm evidence of extraterrestrial involvement. They think aliens helped kill everyone on Earth at the time."

"Right. Last year, one of their geological research teams unearthed this Chaos sample in a quarry near the Lima city-state. Lucky for us, we had subcontracted with the WU to assist. Actually, I can't say it's all luck. I volunteered our services in hopes that they'd make us an official government subcontractor on a permanent basis. Once I got word the team found a substance they couldn't identify, I had my people contain it before the WU got wind and brought the entire drilling team here to Seattle for observation. Three of our crew were exposed to Chaos during the process."

Exposed. I had visions of biohazard tent cities and quarantine zones. "Were they affected?"

"They were. Unfortunately, even with those NDAs you just signed, Legal doesn't like me to let too much information out. You know how they are." She smiled. "But I can tell you about one—Cedric. He was the first to present symptoms, if you can call them that. Cedric led the team that first found Chaos buried in the rock. At the time, he was under regular treatment for stage-1 lung cancer. We put him under study as soon as we got him off the plane. Those were interesting days, waiting to see what the result of his exposure would be."

Interesting wasn't a word I'm guessing poor Cedric would've used. I recognized the coldness in her description, though.

The only way you could cope sometimes was to pretend you were working with inanimate objects rather than people.

"As part of the study, we monitored the tumor on his lung. In only a few hours, it had shrunk by half. By the next morning, it was gone."

I almost laughed. "As in gone, gone? Chaos eradicated his cancer?"

"In unbelievable time. We haven't found a treatment that could make that sort of a difference in a year, maybe three. Chaos excised the cancerous cells before we could finish all the tests we planned to run. And his eyes, they were different—almost like Chaos had pooled over their surfaces. His case was one of the most incredible things I've ever witnessed. Unfortunately"—her tone soured—"Cedric fell into a coma soon after. We weren't able to draw him out of it."

"Is he here? Can I see him?" If I could study his blood, it might be the key to unlocking the growing mountain of unknowns and hopefully help Cedric at the same time.

Gemma shook her head. "Cedric wasn't able to recover. We sent his body back to his family a few weeks ago."

"I'm sorry. I'm sure that was difficult." I wanted to see his file, but I figured it wasn't the right time to ask.

She looked at the sample behind the glass. "Thankfully, not everyone interacts with Chaos the same way. We can't find a pattern to it all hence the name. That's where you come in, Zoe. I need you to unlock this. What it's capable of…I wish I could tell you. You know the alien woman, Prism, we made contact with earlier this year?"

"I do." It was all the news could talk about for months, and with good reason—she was our first visitor from another planet. I even followed the social accounts someone made for her.

"You look at someone like her, who can encase herself in flames and change her body's density, and you think humanity could never measure up. Life outside our planet is beyond us.

But Chaos has given some of our subjects abilities that would make hers look prehistoric by comparison. That's all I can say."

None of what I'd witnessed in the last half hour seemed possible, least of all discussing how human beings could have powers given to them by some scientifically impossible element. I stared blankly at the Chaos canister and tried to make sense of what I knew so far. We had people exposed that either gained unheard of abilities or died from exposure. We had a substance with the potential to create infinite amounts of itself. It was like a plague waiting to happen, one that could either enhance human life or take it.

"What do you think?" Gemma asked.

"We have to figure out a way to control it," I said, "because right now, it's a bomb that no one knows how to diffuse. That's where I want to start—by finding out the inner workings."

Gemma nodded. "Are you up for this challenge?"

I took a deep breath. "I'll do my best."

"I know you will," she replied. She turned and smiled toward the sample. "One thing's for sure—it won't be boring."

CHAPTER THREE

THE CHILLS BROUGHT on by my breezy walk during lunch hadn't faded by the time I returned to my desk. No more HR videos or lab orientations—it was time to start the real work of understanding Chaos's patterns. Like a prize fighter staring me down across the ring, Chaos roiled in its tube behind the protective divider. I only sort of wanted to vomit. To settle down, I reminded myself that I'd done this before. I knew how to handle myself in a lab where I was studying something with a tendency to kill people. Every piece of equipment and every notebook was arranged exactly how I wanted. The only thing left to do was to put my hand over the clean room's palm scanner. I hesitated. It felt like taking a very large step off a very tall cliff.

Come on, Zoe. It only put a guy in a coma once. How bad could it be?

"Having second thoughts?"

I turned around to see Gemma in the doorway.

"It's okay. I figured you might be." The lab door slid shut behind her. She sat down in my chair and rearranged some of the notebooks I'd set out. I felt a twinge of annoyance that she'd messed up my reporting system.

I didn't have the nerve to tell her that I preferred to work alone. Maybe once we'd worked together longer, I could, but for now, I had to let it slide. "I was just about to head in to grab a sample."

"Perfect timing then. And don't mind me—I'm your assistant for the afternoon, that's all. I'll get back to doing paperwork in my office tomorrow."

I tried smiling to brush off the added pressure and held it for a beat too long. An awkward pause followed that widened as I fumbled for a way to interrupt it. "Time to science," I said —for some reason. I even clapped my hands. A coma was starting to sound preferable.

It took three tries to fix my hazmat helmet into the grooved ring around my neck. I could picture Gemma's disappointment in seeing my trembling hands. "I think I'm going to stop drinking morning coffee," I said.

"Let's not make promises we can't keep. I'll buzz you in when you're ready."

I locked the helmet into place and gave a thumbs up over my shoulder. The blood rushing through my ears was almost as loud as the burst of air coming from the decontamination fan above the door. Below my feet, an intake vent sucked in air at the same time, creating a vertical wind tunnel. I knew nothing could get through the material of my suit, but that wasn't much comfort when it felt like I was about to dive into a pool full of acid. As I stepped inside, I tried to remind myself that there was an equal amount of excitement that went along with the fear. I was heading into a room with the unexplained, as much an explorer as I was a molecular biologist.

To avoid contamination, the Chaos sample's container had an automatic process to extract vials for study. I knew that because I'd obsessively read through the lab orientation manual the night before while I battled the insomnia gods. I pressed a few commands on the console screen embedded in the forearm of my suit to get the extraction started. The top of the cylinder rotated, exposing a small opening. After a few seconds, a metal vial around the size of a cigar popped out. It had clear windows on either side for my microscope to see through.

Just like Gemma said, it didn't appear that the main sample had any missing at all. I held the vial up to my helmet to get a closer look. Inside, the Chaos swirled, hypnotic in motion.

I mentally weighed a few opening observations for my logs, which would translate to the paper I'd have to write one day. Everything I came up with bordered on hyperbole. All I could think of was the sample of Chaos moved as if it sought to fulfill a purpose. Like it was searching for something.

What is it you need, I wonder?

As if in answer, my vision shifted.

I wavered on my feet, suddenly dizzy and grasping for mental purchase as I tried to make sense of the rush of adrenaline overwhelming me. The motion sickness gave way to a rumbling in my bones like an earthquake. I stopped everything and widened my stance to weather the tremors. I put my free hand down on the lab table, expecting it to feel like grabbing a running engine, but it didn't register a vibration at all, even though I could feel the quake in every muscle in my body. I shifted my eyes to the vial in my grip.

As I stared at it, waiting for it to fall even though I held it with all my strength, my vision shook again. The room separated into a cascade of repeating images, as though I'd stretched out reality and sliced it like bread.

Then, like an avalanche settling into a valley, the storm stopped. The quaking in my body faded. My dizziness subsided as my vision became whole again.

"Everything okay in there?" Gemma's voice came over the room's speaker.

I took a step back to try to get my breathing under control.

As a hypochondriac kid, my first therapist told me to compare any symptoms I was worried about to symptoms of anxiety, and if they matched up, it was just my head playing tricks. Accordion vision definitely wasn't on the list. The rest of it was, though—elevated heart rate, shallow breathing, the feeling of the world squeezing you on all sides until you burst.

My hypochondriac test once again announced a diagnosis of anxiety. I felt the sting of embarrassment that I'd let my fears build up over the last few weeks to the point that it boiled over so easily. Minus extra points for doing it in front of my new boss.

"Zoe?"

"I'm good," I replied, forgetting that she'd said something. "Probably just should've had food with my coffee this morning. Thinking through my test plan now."

I didn't dare look back to see if she'd bought my story. I still held the vial of Chaos in my right hand, the fingers under my glove sore from gripping it during the panic. For an instant, I wondered if maybe the Chaos had somehow leaked through to my suit and triggered the attack, but that was ridiculous. Every drop of it spun like a cyclone in the vial.

Maybe I'll leave this little episode out of my logs.

"Coming back out," I announced.

The inside of the clean room had a small door beneath the glass divider where I could place the sample for transfer to my equipment on the other side. Gemma watched as I slid it into the compartment.

Another burst of cleansing air doused my suit as I emerged from the Chaos study chamber. I shed the hazmat suit and grabbed my Valhalla lab coat from the wall hook.

Gemma pushed her chair away from my desk to make room for me. "Everything alright? You had me worried for a second."

"I'm okay, I promise," I said. "First day nerves."

She was nice enough to smile. "What's your first step then?"

"Electron microscope," I replied.

"I'll get it ready for you."

Gemma tapped some commands on the virtual keyboard, and the vial disappeared into a tube to be scanned by the microscope. I welcomed the mental shift in focus. Chaos may not have been made of any elements we knew about, but it was made of *something*, and I needed to see for myself what it was.

I took my seat in front of the largest of the three console screens on my desk. The LED interface glowed under my fingers. Adapting to a virtual touchpad came pretty easily, and maneuvering the sample into view was as easy as dragging my finger around. I held my breath as the image came to life. Once the internal lenses of the microscope worked out the focus regions, the picture came into view, revealing a network of web-like threads dotted with red nodules. Orbs of yellow light moved along the paths like electrical signals across neurons. I'd never seen anything like it. The threads were so tiny. At this level of magnification, a single water molecule would take up the entire display. Its bonds would be as thick as my arm. The web that made up Chaos was no bigger than the line of pixels it occupied on screen.

"Beautiful, isn't it?" Gemma said. "What do you think those nodes are?"

"I don't know." But what, exactly, did I know? Chaos wasn't going to show up on the list of periodic elements, so there was no use running a bunch of tests that repeated the work Gemma's crew had already done. Maybe figuring out the behavioral pattern wasn't just about viewing the substance's make-up.

"We could introduce a few reagents," I said. "See how well it plays with others."

"Yeah, we could." The dip in her inflection made it seem like she wasn't impressed with the idea.

"Or we could skip straight to dessert?" I said quickly to try to recover.

"What do you mean?"

Might as well make a big splash on the first day. "Do we have any human tissue samples?" I asked.

Gemma rapped her fingernails on the arm of her chair, pausing just long enough to make me question whether I pushed too far. "We're supposed to register our intent before we use anything from the stem cell line, but… Hold on." She grabbed a set of keys from her bag and slipped out the lab door. A minute later, she came back, carrying a white box.

"You take these," she said, handing the box to me. "They're left over from a drug trial. Lots of subject variance, so you'll get a good mix. I'll run interference on the security system so Anjo doesn't have a conniption about compliance audits."

While she worked on a separate screen, I typed in a command to shift the Chaos sample to the manual interaction chamber, which had rubber gloves attached that I could slip my hands into. I grabbed a handful of the lab slides, including skin cells, blood, and lung tissue to start, and placed them inside the chamber along with some pipettes to transfer the sample. My heart galloped like a thoroughbred in my chest at the thought of extracting some of the Chaos to infuse the cells, even though it was still behind glass. I guarded myself against another panic attack splitting the room into slices. One was enough, thanks.

I set the first slide into position on the edge of the box where a microscope lens hovered. One end of the Chaos sample tube had a membrane that would allow for extraction. I slipped the pipette through the membrane and removed my thumb to start the vacuum process. Chaos filled the hollow space inside. I pressed my eyes against the microscope lenses and held the Chaos over the slide. Drop by drop, it seeped onto the glass.

And then it disappeared.

I backed away from the lenses to make sure, then added two more drops. No matter how many times I tried, the Chaos entered my field of view, dissipated, then vanished.

Unwilling to believe what I'd just seen, I grabbed another slide of cells and placed it under the microscope. Just like the first sample, the Chaos faded to nothing as soon as it touched the glass.

"No, that can't be."

"What?" Gemma asked.

"It…" I almost told her it disappeared, which was impossible. "It seems to have evaporated."

Gemma scooted closer while I tried two more with the same results. Then, on the fifth slide, something changed. The Chaos blended with the cells, breaking apart to spread itself along my field of view. Like an artist tracing the lines of an image, the Chaos attached to the cell walls, making it look like small lines drawing borders around the walls of the skin cells. When it was done, each cell had a red tinge, but otherwise seemed to be intact.

"Is this view being recorded?" I asked.

Gemma pointed to a playback button on screen. I hit it and instantly got a view of the last 30 seconds of study through the microscope. I looped back through the last five seconds, slowing the video speed and magnifying as much as I could.

"What are you looking for?" Gemma asked.

"I would need a more powerful microscope to know for sure, but it looks like strands of Chaos entered the cell first before attaching to the outside, almost as if it was testing the contents."

Gemma sat back. "We haven't seen that before."

My thoughts turned immediately to the man Gemma

spoke of, Cedric, the one who fell into the coma with the red tint to his eyes. Not everyone exposed to the sample showed symptoms, but he had, just like some of my samples were unaffected except the last.

I needed to know whether the man's cells matched what I was seeing under the microscope. If I could see how live cells interacted with it, maybe I could get a better idea of how Chaos worked and why it chose its hosts the way it did. Just thinking the word *hosts* made me shiver. I swiveled to ask about Cedric, but the question came to a halt at the tip of my tongue.

Gemma stared at the screen with tears in her eyes. She looked exhausted, like she'd been trying to hold them in for hours and I just hadn't noticed.

She sniffed and wiped her eyes. "You wouldn't have a tissue, would you?"

"As a matter of fact, I do." I always kept some tissues in my desk drawer. It was an old habit. With Britt, a breakdown could occur any second, and I needed something close by to make it look like it never happened. I handed the box to her.

She wiped a finger under her eye, clearing away the last of her tears. "I just get a dust allergy thing every once in a while. You'd think our offices would be cleaner than this."

The way she forced a smile tugged at my memories, a familiar, painful rendition of the performances I'd given so many times. She was trying so hard to deflect, as if nothing I'd seen should be acknowledged.

"Why don't we take a break," I said. "I can pick up where I left off later."

"No, no. I'm okay."

A struggle played out on her face, where she seemed to have reigned in her sadness, only to have it swell once more. Eventually, she relented, and the tears came again. She grabbed another tissue and lowered her head. "I can't imagine what you must be thinking."

"It's nothing I'd ever judge. I know what it's like." I wanted to roll back time as soon as I said it. She didn't need to know my horrid past. Instead, I pivoted the conversation back to her. "Is there anything I can help with?"

She looked lost before smiling weakly to herself. "As a matter of fact, it's why I hired you."

"Oh?"

Gemma looked up as if she'd just woken from a dream. "No, I meant—oh never mind. I might as well tell you. Better it comes from me than the usual office gossip. You're not the first person who's caught me crying at work."

I wasn't sure I wanted to be in this conversation. It had been easy to get along with Gemma so far, but it seemed like she was about to take it to a level of familiarity I avoided with colleagues. If they opened up to me, there was a danger I could feel comfortable enough to open up to them—and that meant risking Britt's wrath if she found out. I couldn't decide if it was more inappropriate to walk out or stay.

"My daughter is sick," Gemma said. "About ten months ago, she was diagnosed with an aggressive form of cancer. We treated it the best we could, but it spread to her brain. When I saw the cells on your screen just now, it reminded me of seeing her biopsy results for the first time."

"Oh, I'm so sorry. I can't imagine." I instantly felt bad for wanting out of the conversation.

"We pinned our hopes on some experimental drugs early on to control the growth, but we'd started them too late. The swelling got to the point where her body shut down. She's been non-responsive for the last three months. No signs that she'll recover. The hospital has a policy that without a certain amount of brain activity after a period of time, they remove life support. They want to do it next week."

There was nothing I could do to make it better, so I didn't try. "What's her name?" I asked instead.

"Amaryn."

"It's beautiful. I love it."

Gemma smiled. "Her father was something of an ancient history buff. We couldn't agree on a name—he wanted Amara, and I wanted Meryn—so we combined them. It worked out, unlike our marriage. He left when Amaryn was two. She was the best gift he ever gave me, honestly, although you'd never know it to look at us. Amaryn has always had something of a quick temper, which she gets from me. Our fights have gone on for days, sometimes. I lost count of how many times she's told me she hated me—especially since she's been out of high school. She and I were at each other's throats right up until the day she got diagnosed. All of a sudden, she was my little girl again. She even let me hug her." Gemma wiped another tear away. "Sorry. I don't mean to go on."

"No, it's okay. Sounds like she was special."

"She still is." It was a curt response. She sat back against the chair and straightened up like she was willing herself to regain professional distance. "Anyway, my hope is that I can keep the hospital from giving up on her while you continue your research into Chaos. To be honest, it's why I wanted to sit in with you. I needed a sense of how quickly you work. We've already seen how Chaos cured Cedric's cancer. If we can isolate the means by which it can do something like that, we can use it to ease her symptoms—and others like her."

All of a sudden, the weight of my research doubled. I didn't want to give her false hope, especially since it was so early and I had way more questions than answers—not to mention the fact that human trials were likely years away. I tried to think of a good way to temper her expectations.

"This has been a great start, but—"

My phone chimed again. *Does the WU have me on butt speed dial?* I glanced at the screen and lost any ability to complete my sentence. The number listed was Unknown. It had a single word in the text.

Seattle?

She'd found me.

"Oh no… *No!*" I shot out of my chair.

Gemma got up and walked to my side. "Zoe? What's wrong?"

It felt like Britt was already in the room with me, already accusing me of cheating on her, of wanting to hurt her.

And how she was going to hurt me right back.

"Zoe!"

I gasped at the sound of my name, expecting Britt to be the one standing in front of me yelling instead of Gemma. She guided me back down to the chair and put her hand on my shoulder. "It's okay," she said. "You're okay."

I realized I wasn't breathing. I let the air out of my chest and immediately began to thirstily drink in breaths as if I might drown any second. "She found me."

"Who found you?"

"I'm not safe here."

"Yes, you are. This building is the safest place you could be."

I wanted to cry, not out of sadness, but defeat. I'd taken my best shot at leaving Britt behind, and it was all for nothing. I could never escape her. Ever.

Gemma got up and tapped the screen by the office door. The internal locks engaged. "There," she said. "No one can get in here, and the walls are sound shielded. Tell me what's going on."

She spoke so calmly, like she'd spent years dealing with people in crisis. When I looked up at her leaning forward in her chair, I didn't see judgment or even a hint she wanted to be free of the situation. She looked at me like she genuinely cared.

Britt's resurgent voice in my head reminded me that no one cared. No one could help.

"I'm sorry," I said. "I overreacted. I'm okay."

"With all due respect, Zoe, that's bullshit." She handed me

one of my tissues. "I know I'm just your boss and you barely know me, but I know a thing or two about keeping my problems inside. Let's call this a temporary dismantling of the manager/employee wall. You'll feel better if you get it out of your system."

I felt like that wall had already been demolished. Maybe she was right, though. "It's my ex," I said.

She nodded as if I'd told her everything with just those three words. "Now I see why you moved so far away."

"I didn't tell a soul where I was going, or even that I was leaving. I planned it for months. My old lab manager let me quit without announcing it so Britt wouldn't find out from any of our friends at work until I was gone."

"Do you think they told her?"

"I don't know. Brandon was the only person I trusted. Britt always made it a point to become friends with everyone I knew. It's how she kept track of me when I wasn't around. Brandon hated her, though. He saw through her right away. When she figured out she couldn't make him one of her spies, Britt accused me of cheating with him."

"I see. One of those."

"The *queen* of 'those.' I thought I'd done everything right. I thought I could start new here."

"Listen," Gemma said, kneeling down until she looked me in the eye. "Everything you did to get here took a lot of courage. You *have* started new. I know a lot of people in this town, including people who could make sure Britt never steps foot in Seattle if we don't want her to."

It was a nice thought. It would never happen, though. If a protection order wasn't enough to keep her away before, no amount of threatening was ever going to work.

"I'll tell you a story," Gemma said. "You remember I mentioned Amaryn's dad?"

I nodded.

"His name was Felix. Felix wasn't exactly keen on the idea

of having kids when we met, but it was something I told him was important to me before we got married. We had Amaryn not too long after we moved here. He started out okay after she was born, but it wasn't long before he started staying out later at work and making excuses to go in on weekends. By the time she was two, I'd had enough of being a single parent. I got one of my friends to watch Amaryn one night, and I went down to the bar where I knew he was a regular. Sure enough, he and his buddies were sitting in a booth, so drunk they didn't notice me. I pulled him out of his seat and let him have it right in front of everyone in the bar. That's when he hit me." She tapped her jaw. "Right here."

"That's awful," I said. It was also familiar.

"My face was purple by the time I got home. When I looked at myself in the mirror, all I could see was him doing the same to Amaryn one day. I couldn't stand the thought of it. I waited in our living room with the lights out for Felix to come home. When he came through the door, I hit him with his favorite hammer." She pointed to her jaw again. "Right here."

"You weren't scared of his reaction?"

"Anger can be a good motivator. While he was on the floor, crying like the baby he never wanted, I told him if I ever saw him again, that hammer was gonna be aimed a few inches higher. I kicked him out and then sold his stuff the next day. I also called in a favor with a friend of mine in the Security Office at the World Union. Felix didn't know it, but his job was about to transfer him to a remote region east of Moscow. He was also told that if he ever set foot back in Seattle, he'd find himself on a one-way trip to Tartarus, and not with the comfy prison pajamas."

I smiled despite the widening pit of anxiety in my stomach. "What happened to him?"

"I know he bought a lot of coats, but more importantly, I never saw him again." She straightened up and leaned against my desk. "I didn't tell you this because you need to go buy a hammer, Zoe. I said it because it is possible to protect you from this Britt person. I still have that friend at the WU."

I didn't want to tell her that Britt would be the one hiding in the dark with a hammer. I'd said too much already. I just wanted to rewind time and never bring my boss into this.

"I'm sure I'm overreacting," I said. "It probably wasn't her, anyway."

"Zoe…"

"It's okay, I promise." I got up and headed for the door. "I'm gonna go get some air."

"Wait," Gemma said. "Can I see your phone?"

I passed my phone to her and waited while she made a few taps on the screen.

"You've got my personal number now," she said. "If you don't feel safe—or even if you just want to talk about things— you call me. I'll pick up, day or night."

"I don't want to wake you with my crazy worries."

"You won't. I don't sleep much when I'm at the hospital." She leaned in and gave me a hug. "I mean it, Zoe. You call me."

I mumbled a goodbye and nearly ran to the elevator. All I wanted was to get out of there and start planning my next escape.

CHAPTER FOUR

THE WALK down to the waterfront was supposed to chip away at the shock of Britt's text. It did, sort of, but you couldn't drain an ocean with an eyedropper.

At one point, the idea that I was surrounded by a city of millions gave me confidence I could stay hidden, but now, even in the masses, it was hard not to see Britt everywhere. Every corner was a potential ambush. Every footstep behind me was the precursor to an attack. What I needed was something to clear a path through my fears so I could see a way out of this hell. Wine usually did the trick. A glass or two would do it.

Or ten, just to be sure.

I thought about calling my parents. I even went so far as to pull up their number, but I couldn't bring myself to make the call. I could already hear the disappointment in their voices. I wasn't the daughter they imagined I'd be. It had taken so many awkward, forced dinners at the house before they accepted Britt—or rather, accepted that I had chosen her. They didn't think she was good enough for me, whatever that meant. As much as I loved my mother, she'd always held to the theory that any speck of dirt on your clothes meant they were ready for the thrift box. Britt wasn't a concert violinist or a surgeon. She didn't measure up, and therefore, she could only bring me down. It wasn't just the shame of failing that kept me from dialing the number—it was like an admission that they were right and I wasn't the person I was before. She'd ruined me. I was to be tossed in a box, ready for the thrift tags.

On impulse, I bought a ticket to a movie and sat in silence near the back. I don't even know what it was about, but it was enough of a distraction to continue deadening my nerves. By the time I got out, the sun was already dipping below the Olympics. The streets by the docks were mercifully quiet. While I didn't need my earbuds with the hypnotic sounds of Cascade Bay so close, I kept them in anyway. The familiar white noise was a crutch I was all too ready to lean on. Most of the restaurants by the water were meant for tourists. In a way, I still was one. Nothing about their neon signs or muffled pop music screamed *safety* to me though. Instead, I looked around for something smaller, somewhere I could be left alone to figure out what to do next.

I found an Italian place called Roma's on Front Street that was only distinguishable from the shadows by a dim yellow light over a menu board. The lone bad review I found online came from someone complaining about the lack of seating for big parties. Small, quiet, and sure to have bottomless cabernet.

Perfect.

Aside from the cheap wooden sign hanging above Roma's, the rest of the street was a canvas of darkness. All of the tension I'd shed returned in a rush. I felt like a kid again staring down the black abyss at the bottom of my grandparent's basement stairs. I took out my earbuds before I stepped into the shadows. I wanted to be on alert, no matter how badly the sounds of the city needled my anxiety. I still had 911 programmed as the quick call on my phone, and I held my finger over the button as I walked with my hand in my pocket.

Each step felt like disturbing the silk of a spider's web. I held my breath until the moment I rushed through the restaurant's door. The waitstaff looked at me like I was on fire. I felt like it.

"Is this table taken?" I asked, pointing to the small two-seater by the window. The hostess grabbed a menu and walked me to it. Sitting there pretty much guaranteed I'd be watching for monsters in the shadows instead of eating, but I couldn't bring myself to sit in the back. There was no exit except through the kitchen. I'd be trapped.

I can't keep thinking like this, or I'll drive myself crazy. She's not here.

I glanced outside at the empty street.

Not yet, anyway.

I ordered the first thing on the menu I saw that had carbs. Carbs were delicious and well-known for keeping a girl full when she meant to stay up all night worrying about being strangled. I also ordered an espresso instead of the wine I craved. Maybe some caffeine could induce a heart attack to cap off the evening.

The place turned out to be exactly what I hoped it would be. The staff mostly left me alone, and the food was delicious. My nervous stomach gave me enough of a break to eat a few bites in relative peace. I only almost threw up twice.

The waitress came to check on me after my meal had long since grown cold. "Need anything else, hon?"

Hon. I hadn't been called that since my trip through the southern city-states as a kid. "Just the bill, thanks."

"You want a to-go box for your leftovers?"

I didn't, but the people-pleaser in me couldn't bring myself to refuse. "That would be great."

I went back to looking through the restaurant's front window while I waited. The street remained quiet. I'd made it through half a day since the text, and not a single terrifying scenario my brain had concocted had come true. I could almost feel some of the knots in my shoulders start to unwind.

Then, a woman's silhouette turned off Front Street toward Roma's. She was about my height, wearing jeans and a red and black checkered shirt with the sleeves rolled up halfway. It was an outfit I'd seen a thousand times.

I leaned over to make sure. My chest rose and fell in quick breaths. I couldn't make out her face in the dark, but she walked exactly like Britt—methodical in each slow step, as if she knew she'd catch me no matter how fast I ran.

By trying to get a better look, I'd waited too long to escape. I didn't know what to do. She was almost to the door.

I jumped out of my chair, scaring the waitress so much she spilled my box of leftovers on the floor.

I fumbled for the phone in my pocket, finally finding the quick call button. I held it down and waited for the police to pick up.

"World Union Seattle, what's your emergency?" a man on the other end answered.

"I'm at Roma's near the waterfront!" I nearly screamed. "My name is Zoe Daniel. My ex is about to attack me. Her name is Britt Spencer."

"Okay, are you somewhere safe?"

The waitress looked from me to the cook in the back, confused.

Britt was only seconds away from coming inside, I could feel it. I pushed past the waitress to get to the entrance. Just as my nightmare was about to grab the handle, I slammed the lock on the door and held the latch down.

We saw each other as she stepped into the light of the restaurant's sign. Me, panting from fear and wavering on my feet. Her, a complete stranger. A woman now as terrified as me.

Oh gods.

"Ma'am?" the voice on the line said.

I backed away from the door, still in horror at what I'd done. The lady on the other side—who looked nothing like Britt at all—disappeared into the darkness to escape the crazed woman staring back at her.

I'd never been so embarrassed. My waitress stared at me with wide eyes.

"I'm sorry," I muttered into the phone before cutting the line. I unlocked the front door and left in a near sprint. The waitress came out after me, shouting into the street that she'd tell the cops I stiffed them for the bill.

I ran until I didn't know where I was anymore. All I wanted to do was collapse on my bed and cry, but I was too far from home to do it. Instead, I found a bench outside of the downtown library and buried my face in my jacket as I wept. I must have looked like a fool. I felt like one. I hated Britt for so many reasons, but the thing I hated her for most was turning me into someone I didn't recognize.

My phone buzzed in my pocket. I audibly gasped, causing a man walking by to give me a wide berth. I didn't want to look at the screen at first. I pulled it out anyway, driven by the same perverse urge as looking over a canyon edge to see how far you'd fall.

A text from Gemma glowed bright on the screen: *You make it home okay?*

My fingers hovered over the keyboard. This was my boss, not my mom and not my buddy. I shouldn't be burdening the person whose opinion of me could make or break my career.

Who cares if it does? I can't keep going like this.

I thought about what she said in her office—about how she knew someone who could make sure Britt never threatened me again. I wondered if Gemma could really give me the security she promised.

I texted back before I lost my nerve: *Not home yet. Managed to make a fool out of myself on the way. I thought I saw Britt.*

Seconds stretched on without a reply. I almost threw the phone into traffic out of embarrassment.

Then the phone buzzed again: *Where are you?*

I looked around until I saw a street sign: *Library on 8th*

Good. You're close. Come by the hospital, three blocks down on Fairview, room 417.

The voice in my head telling me this wasn't something I should involve my boss in still clamored, but it quickly faded to a whisper. The amount of relief I felt just reading Gemma's words was like a blanket over a fire. I checked the map on my phone and set off to meet her.

ENTERING the hospital lobby was another layer of much-needed security I needed to calm myself. It helped being around people whose job it was to look after others. It wasn't until I saw a patient walking down the main hallway with their IV tower in one hand that I came out of my cocoon of self-pity and remembered that Gemma was here for her daughter. All of a sudden, the weight of my problems took a back seat to crippling embarrassment again. *This woman doesn't need my problems, too.*

"Need help?" a woman asked. She wore a sweater over her nurse's uniform.

I realized I'd been staring at the fire hose beside the elevator. "Sorry, just trying to remember the room."

"We have a map by the front desk if you need it."

"That's okay. Thank you." It was too late for second guessing now. Gemma might call the cops if I didn't at least make an appearance. I pressed the button and jumped on the elevator. No matter what happened, I planned to crawl into a hole at the office and never see Gemma or anyone else again for weeks after this night was over.

After a maddening few seconds of elevator motor noise, the bell dinged for the fourth floor. When I stepped out, I wondered if maybe I'd hit the wrong button. It wasn't until I saw a small light on at the nurse's station down the dark hallway that I could tell there was anyone in the ward at all. It was like walking into a library after closing—a library owned by insanely rich people. The walls were a smooth wood, stained a brassy shade, with digital pads installed beside each door displaying patient information and service links. The screens gave off a faint warm glow as I walked down the carpeted hall.

I knocked softly when I got to room 417. Gemma opened the door and immediately greeted me with a hug. It had been so long, I'd forgotten I was a hugger.

"I'm glad you're safe," she said.

She stepped back to let me into the room, giving way to a small living area complete with a fridge, TV, and couch. Her daughter's treatment room was behind a closed door on the back wall. Gemma looked like she'd been sleeping.

"I'm really sorry," I said. "I shouldn't be bothering you while you're here with Amaryn."

Gemma scoffed. "Nonsense. You caught me before I was about to leave." She sat down on the couch and patted the seat next to her. "Tell me what happened."

I was on the couch and telling her the whole series of events before I knew it. Somehow, it was more embarrassing re-telling the story than it was living it. I didn't think that was possible. I ended it with the exciting conclusion of my public breakdown on the library bench.

"You're on edge for good reason," she said. "But you're

safe now. When we're done here, we can share a taxi back to your place. I'll drop you off before I head home."

"Thank you," I said. "You don't have to do that."

"It's nothing. I know you'd do the same if the roles were reversed."

Just the thought of Gemma calling me for a favor outside of work seemed off, almost like a teacher wanting to hang out with me after school.

"You want to see her?" she asked, pointing to her daughter's room.

I looked at Amaryn's door. "Oh no. I couldn't."

"Why not?"

"I…I don't know. It seems too private."

"Gods, not at all." Gemma got up and walked toward Amaryn's door. The way she did it so confidently, it was clear she meant for me to follow.

I did, only because I couldn't add "offending my boss" to an already stressful night. Gemma led the way. The room was dark save for the street light filtering through closed curtains and a few blinking readouts on the instruments. She stopped at the end of the bed and waited for me to come in. Little by little, Amaryn's bed revealed itself as I walked into the room, and with it, the frail outline of her body beneath the blankets.

I had to keep myself from gasping when I saw her. I was supposed to be used to such a thing, after all. Working in bio research, this was a scene I'd become familiar with, but it somehow always felt like the first time. You never got used to seeing the human body in such advanced decline.

The cancer had eaten away most of her. She looked like she might've been slightly taller than I was and yet she couldn't have weighed more than a hundred pounds. The machines around her bed took up more room than she did. There was an auto-breather, an IV fluid regulator, two separate heart monitors, and a blood particulate monitor.

Gemma approached her bedside softly, as if she might wake her. She stroked Amaryn's thin brown hair out of her face.

The analytical part of me knew right away why the hospital wanted to make the call to end Amaryn's life. The hardware in the room must have cost thousands of dollars a day to maintain. The machines weren't meant for this level of care. Then, there was Amaryn. She was a withered husk of a person. I didn't have to look at her chart to know she wouldn't last a second without the aid of machines.

And I only had to look at Gemma to understand why she fought.

It wasn't that she didn't understand her daughter's situation, I imagined, it was that she didn't want to accept that it couldn't be solved. I knew that feeling and recognized the dogged determination immediately. It's how I'd reacted to every challenge in my career. I'd stay in the lab for hours until I got the result I knew was possible, and sometimes I'd look exactly as she did now—weathered and starved for energy but determined despite it all.

"She's better today, I think," Gemma said.

I nodded, wondering how that could be possible.

"Ever since she was diagnosed, we broke things down into little battles, you know? Lower an indicator by a decimal, shrink a tumor by a millimeter, keep a spoonful of food down… Today, that battle is to keep some of her color. I think there's a bit of red in her cheeks since yesterday."

"That's great," I replied.

Gemma smiled at me over her shoulder before going back to stroking Amaryn's hair. "She's going to be nineteen in a few days. If I can sneak them past that witch of a nurse down at the station, I'm going to bring in some oatmeal cookies for her to smell. They're her favorite."

It was heartbreaking to think about what Gemma had gone through up until this point. The way she looked at her daughter, you could feel the connection between them. I wasn't used to seeing genuine affection in people. It felt foreign. My instinct was to deny it as being real, but I had to remind myself that there were caring people in the world, people who legitimately wanted the best for others. Who loved them.

It wasn't weird or strange that Gemma kept offering to help me. That's who she was. She actually cared.

All of a sudden, I felt the urge again—the urge to solve the problem everyone else said couldn't be solved. It had to be possible to reverse Amaryn's condition. There had to be something the doctors overlooked.

Or something they didn't know existed.

Chaos.

It was the reason why Gemma hired me, as she said. There were no such things as miracles, but that didn't mean Chaos couldn't do extraordinary things. My mind raced. Maybe there was a way we could use it to treat Amaryn's disease on a cellular level, perhaps through dialysis. I started thinking of treatment methods and schedules. All I needed to get started was a hint of how the substance worked. I'd already seen how it spread into a cell. If I could find out how it changed the cell's make-up—how it manifested certain abilities—I could steer it to do what I wanted.

I could help cure her.

"I should go," I said.

"Are you sure?" Gemma stood and walked to my side. "I still owe you that ride to your apartment."

"Actually, I think I'm headed back to the lab."

"Zoe… You can't work all hours."

"Just for a bit," I said. "Promise."

"Okay," she said with a smile. "If you're sure." She looked back at her daughter before adding, "There's a car waiting for me downstairs. I'll let them know they should take you to the office."

"Thank you."

"Call me if you need me. For anything," she added.

I gave Amaryn one final look to cement my motivation before I left. The familiar rush of finding a puzzle to solve had taken hold. I almost floated down the elevator on my way out to the car.

And somehow, in all of it, I'd managed to forget about Britt, at least for a little while.

Just hold on, Amaryn. You've got another person fighting for you now.

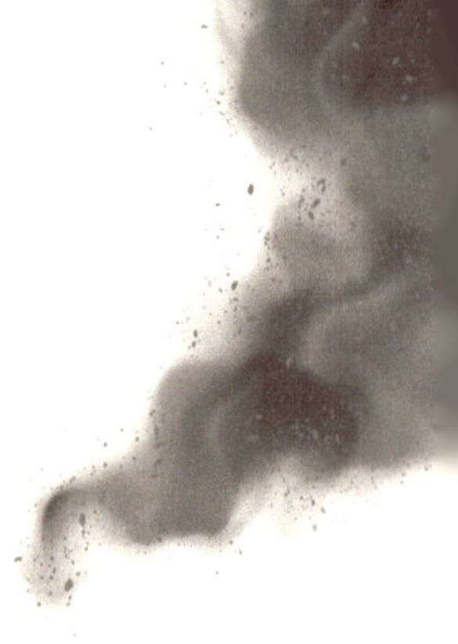

CHAPTER FIVE

A MONSTER STOOD in wait behind every shadow on the way to the Valhalla building, and I managed to ignore them all. I couldn't even remember placing my hand on the scanner when I got on the elevator. I was an explorer at the spring of an unexplored river. Gods, I'd missed that feeling.

The labs were blissfully silent. I walked so fast, my hastily gathered ponytail bounced in rhythm against the back of my neck. As fast as my mind raced, I did my best to corral enough thoughts to piece together a test plan. The first step was to get a fresh sample from the Chaos canister. The fact that it could replicate on its own was a pharmaceutical dream come true. Whatever delivery method I might develop, I simply had to wait for the compound to refill itself before continuing with any treatment. One canister could be used for an entire hospital full of patients. The possibilities were almost too big to think about. This was a potential treasure trove of medical advancement.

And I was at the forefront.

I slid through the door of my hidey-hole lab and quickly shed my jacket to grab a hazmat suit, typing in the commands to produce a Chaos sample while I slipped the suit on. I left the hood for last, making sure I had my earphones in with the white noise playing. I wanted no distractions, not even the rumbling heartbeat of the ventilation system.

While I sealed the fasteners of my hood in place, I started to formulate the first mini goal of the night. My initial thought was to isolate the moments after Chaos attached to our cells. If I could just get a picture of those first few milliseconds of interaction—or better yet, a hi-res recording I could watch in slow motion—I could set myself up for an even bigger day the next morning.

But who was I kidding? I wasn't going home, not with so much momentum behind me. It was going to be a steady stream of coffee and vending machine muffins until Gemma carted me out of there. No use fooling myself with an oasis of healthy choices.

When I stepped into the clean room and the door shut behind me, I conjured as much focus as my racing mind could muster while the sampling system worked. I'd already lost some of my jitteriness about being around Chaos and had to remind myself repeatedly that this stuff was capable of horrible things as well as good. The story of Cedric was proof of that. I wanted Amaryn's story to have a happier ending.

The swirling red substance filled the glass tube like a rising thermometer. I couldn't wait to grab it and fill a syringe.

Then the top of the Chaos container moved.

I didn't want to believe it was real. I wanted the subtle shift I witnessed out of the corner of my eye to be the movement of a shadow instead of the beginning of a containment breach. The stinging scrape of metal cemented the nightmare as reality. A probing strand of Chaos crept through the opening like an animal realizing its cage had been left open. I reached up to close the container as fast as I could, but the bulkiness of my hazmat suit betrayed me, knocking the cap free as I tried to grab it. The top clattered to the floor. The strand of Chaos widened to a stream at the sound, then swelled over the sides in a rushing waterfall.

I fumbled at the console on my sleeve. The oversized fingers of my gloves might as well have been concrete blocks. I couldn't take hold of the screen. Once I did, I tapped furiously on the icons, keeping one eye on the expanding flood of Chaos coming over the side of the cylinder. I hit the icon to start the emergency ventilation system.

Nothing happened.

"No!" I screamed. I hit the button repeatedly, but the system wouldn't trigger.

I have to get out of here. My only hope for containment was to lock the room from my office console. I turned to run and found myself staring at a cloud of swirling Chaos.

The substance looked even more alien outside of its confines, its surface like a rippling red sea made up of writhing worms. The cloud expanded slowly, methodically— purposefully. A single red tendril emerged from the hovering mass, searching like a blind predator surrounded by bleeding prey. The end of the protrusion split into claw-like wisps that slipped over my forearm. In an already compact room with more of the Chaos behind me, I thrashed to break free, which only entangled me in its net more, and I ended on my knees while I batted at the red wave coating my glove like it was a spreading fire. The probing arms persisted, separating and joining back together when I broke through its surface. They closed around the seams of my gloves. I couldn't take a breath no matter how hard I tried. The arm of Chaos hovered over my glove, testing the seams until it managed to seep through the air-tight closure. I screamed behind my face shield. The edges of its fingers brushed against my wrist, an exploratory touch before it plunged beneath my skin in a firestorm of pain.

The cloud of Chaos spawned another searching arm. It reached for my mask.

I got up and ran through the floating sea of red to the lab door on the other side and hit the button to force it open while the Chaos already inside my suit spread over my body. I could feel it absorbing deep into my muscles, an electric burst of heat that dissipated to an unwelcome, steady warmth. More shocking than the horror of what was happening to me was how quickly I gave in to the idea that my time was at an end. I wasn't going to make it out of this.

But that didn't mean I had let Chaos take anyone else.

As the clean room door slammed behind me, I ran to the console and keyed in the sequence to initiate a complete lockdown of my lab. The red, hovering mass lingered in the air where I'd stood, as if it was waiting for me to come back inside so it could finish its work.

My arm shook at my hip. I clumsily unfastened the glove of my opposite hand so I could get the infected part of my suit off faster. I almost tore it from the shoulder trying to get free. I held up my left arm, expecting it to be riddled with spider webs of Chaos.

Nothing.

I turned it back and forth twice. I checked everywhere, looking for signs of redness or inflammation—some evidence that the Chaos had forced its way inside my body and I hadn't imagined the whole thing. There was no trace. I shed the rest of my suit and threw it in the corner piece by piece to make sure the sample hadn't drifted onto other parts of my body. There was no trace. When I looked back into the clean room, the Chaos cloud still sat suspended in air. The tendril that had wrapped itself around my arm looked exactly as it had when I ran out. It hadn't come with me.

I wasn't out of the woods yet, but at least the danger was as contained as I could make it.

I guess I can get those infected blood samples I wanted now.

It was a bad joke, a weak attempt to cool down my fears, but they were well on their way to the boiling point. *How could*

I have been so clumsy? I ran through the list of safety protocols that were pre-programmed to trigger when I entered the lab, which should have included a leak check on the container lid. This kind of equipment failure was unforgivable, bordering on impossible. It had to be my fault. I had missed something simple that should've prevented this.

It didn't matter what Gemma thought of me—my time at Valhalla was at an end. And how could I blame her? It was a mistake I'd expect from a first-year student, not from someone like me. I wanted to cry—not because of the job, and not just because I'd managed to potentially infect myself, but because I knew I'd just wasted a chance to help Amaryn. Her fight had just gotten harder.

I looked at my arm again, running my fingers over the spot where Chaos had broken through.

My mental footing gave way to nauseating dizziness.

A shuddering wave hit me, even stronger than the one I'd felt before during my panic attack. My vision threatened to split into shards again. I grabbed both arms of my desk chair and shut my eyes to ride out the storm. The sensation only worsened. I felt like I was at the epicenter of an earthquake. My fingers dug into the chair's arms. My whole body seemed ready to shatter. I held on as long as I could until the only release from the pain came from a throat-shredding scream.

The internal frenzy stretched on with bursts of hot electricity storming through my arms and legs until I was sure my heart would explode. I finally managed a breath, then another to push back the storm little by little. When the tremors finally faded and the dizziness passed, I kept my eyes closed. I was afraid I'd see the world sliced into cascading panes like before. What I wanted to see was the rest of the lab in shambles so I knew the earthquake wasn't just in my head. I opened my eyes to check. The office looked exactly the same, the world surrounding me still whole.

Through the glass, Chaos watched silently.

I covered my ears as the alarm system sounded from the hallway outside. Sirens blared. The overhead bulbs switched off, replaced by strobing red emergency lights. I could barely think straight under the pressure of the noise.

A rectangle of light hit the console in front of me. I spun around in my chair to see a team of Valhalla security in hazmat suits rushing inside. Two of them grabbed my arm before I could stop them. They held me in my chair while another man passed blue scanners over my body. The last guard headed for the clean room door.

"Stay out of that room!" I shouted over the alarms.

As I sat held in place by security, a fifth person in hazmat gear entered. I couldn't see who it was at first as the particulate reader passed over my eyes. Then I saw her face behind the hood's shield. It was Gemma. She looked furious.

"She's one of us!" she yelled at the security team.

The guards tightened their hold.

Before I knew what was happening, two of the men gripped my upper arms and ripped me out of my chair. I was half-carried, half-led out of the room.

"Gemma?!" I cried out as I was dragged past her. "Where are they taking me?"

"You're okay," she called back. Her hazmat boots thudded in time with the guards as she ran after us. "You're okay, Zoe!"

I could barely breathe. With the lights flashing and the sirens still blaring, my brain was on overload.

After a sharp turn, the men carried me into a dark room and dropped me on the floor. The tile was like ice beneath my fingers. The door shut behind me, leaving me alone. The room fell black. A few seconds later, a dull fluorescent bulb above me flickered, casting a yellow wash on the floor.

At last, the sirens stopped, leaving behind a pulsing echo in my ears. I got up and ran to the door, where a single narrow window stood over the lock mechanism. "Hey!" I yelled. I pounded on the glass. "HEY!"

Gemma's face appeared on the other side. She removed her hood and barked a silent order over her shoulder to the men who'd thrown me in. I couldn't hear a word.

She turned back to me, and for a moment, I had a window into what Amaryn must have seen from behind her frozen stare every day. Gemma looked me over with tired, worried eyes. It was the look of someone who knew the life of the other would never be the same, if there was still life to live.

A speaker next to me clicked on.

"Are you okay?" she asked.

I shook my head. I wasn't okay. I was scared, I was confused, but most of all, I was angry—angry at myself for what I'd let happen.

"I tried," Gemma said. "I tried to think of another way. I got an alert at the hospital that there'd been a breach, and my hands were tied. I had to order the isolation. I'm so sorry, Zoe."

"It's my fault," I answered.

"Don't do that to yourself. We can talk about what happened once you're out, but for now, just relax as much as you can. I'll get you out of this, okay?"

The speaker clicked off again. Gemma smiled as she backed away from the window. It was a smile poorly masking what was going on beneath the surface. I couldn't match her feigned optimism.

I slipped down with my back against the door and buried my face in my hands.

CHAPTER SIX

I DIDN'T SEE anyone for hours, not until a man in a baggy white hazmat suit walked through the burst of decontamination air and fitted me with telemetry receptors before clumsily drawing a vial of blood. He didn't get the tourniquet tight enough.

"You can't keep me here," I said.

The man twisted the cap shut on the vial.

"I want to see Gemma."

He disappeared through the heavy door without answering, leaving me alone again in what looked like an old clean room converted into a cell. The air was heavy with dust and smelled like mold. There was nothing to sit on—no bed or chair, only a simple table against the wall to keep me company.

The solitude was anything but silent. My internal volume was cranked to full, making sure I heard everything—from the crackling of the receptors against my temples when I swallowed to the barely-audible motor whirrs as the security cameras refocused after my every move. I couldn't even stand the sound of my own breathing. I wanted my earbuds so badly.

Another faceless man lumbered through in his hazmat suit a few minutes later. Another vial of my blood walked out with him.

"You should draw more than one at a time," I called after him. "It's more efficient. Asshole."

Although he'd tried to hide it from me, I caught a glimpse of the brown coating at the bottom of the second vial. *Diametrinil.* It was a common reagent, meant to show them immediately if a foreign substance was present in my blood. Crime labs used it all the time to test for drugs. In my case, they had to be looking for Chaos.

Since I was still conscious and not dead or in a coma, I assumed that either I wasn't infected, or Chaos had disappeared from my body like the sample I'd watched under the microscope. The fact that they kept coming back for blood planted an uncomfortable seed of doubt. Maybe I had gotten infected even though I didn't show any epidermal signs. Maybe there was an incubation period and Chaos was about to unveil its plans for me. My mind started to race with unwelcome possibilities. I sat on the floor and hugged my arms to my chest. The room felt colder all of a sudden.

The door to my cell opened, accompanied by the rusted wails of its hinges. It was a guard this time, judging by the neural gun on his hip. A rifle like that had enough voltage to stop a charging rhino. He tossed a stack of papers on the lone table in the room.

"What's that?"

"A reminder," he answered on his way out.

I couldn't stand waiting for someone to tell me whether I was sick or not anymore. It was a miracle I'd been able to keep my anxiety in check so far. *Reading this isn't going to help*, I told myself as I picked up the stack of papers on the table. It wouldn't, but maybe it would keep me from running over the same carousel of doomsday scenarios again and again. Maybe the papers would tell me exactly which of the nightmares I should focus on.

The title page read, *Amendment to Non-Disclosure Agreement*. It was a tome of legal gibberish. I flipped to the last page to see what the point of giving it to me was and saw my signature on the bottom. I took a step back. It was one of the endless stacks of papers I'd signed on my first day.

I went back to the beginning and scanned the first few pages. It was all the standard corporate bullshit I'd seen a million times, but then I saw what the guard meant for me to read, buried halfway through. I didn't have to wonder about Valhalla's plans for me anymore. It was spelled out on paper, clear as day.

I was to be held indefinitely, and I'd agreed to it.

The Chaos "virus," as they called it, was their property, and as such any advancements or results pertaining to the virus were theirs, too. As someone who'd come in contact with it, that meant me. I hurriedly flipped through the rest of the document. Paragraph after paragraph detailed how I was going to be treated during the "isolation phase," which had no documented end. They wanted to see what effect the virus had on me. They wanted me studied. They wanted to control every aspect—including what I might say if I ever spoke to anyone again.

If.

Immediately, I thought about the test subjects Gemma told me about and how I couldn't find any information on them, save for Cedric, and even that was little more than a summary sheet. I hadn't seen any of the patients. Hadn't heard mention of them. It's like they never existed. Now, I was one of them.

I let the stack of papers fall back on the table. The idea that a government or a company could make someone disappear was a myth—something you saw in movies. I couldn't comprehend it. I'd never go outside again. Never see my family. Never walk back into my apartment or leave the building on my own again. I'd seen what the World Union had done to that alien woman they'd found. The only reason she wasn't under lock and key was because she had powers. I had no powers. I was a walking petri dish to be kept sealed in a lab. I'd left La Grange so secretly, no one knew where I was. No one could save me because no one knew I needed to be saved.

I had to get out. I had to show them I wasn't a threat.

Better yet, I thought, *I need to show them that they still need me.*

I ran to the door and started pressing my hand against the keypad, trying anything to get someone's attention.

"Hey!" I yelled into the speaker above it. "I need to talk to Gemma. If I'm infected, I'm your best chance at studying the effects!"

The porthole window remained empty. No one was coming, not even Gemma.

Every muscle in my body tightened. I wanted to tear every page of the NDA apart. I wanted to scream at myself for being so stupid as I replayed the entire failure back in my mind. I even tried, but I couldn't.

I lost the ability to speak as soon as a yellow haze materialized over my skin.

I stumbled back at the sight, hitting the table and knocking the stack of legal work into a shower of paper. The shockwave of dizziness I'd felt earlier in the lab came back in a rush. I closed my eyes and braced myself to hit the floor. Despite the sensation that I'd been thrown down an elevator shaft, I managed to keep my feet under me. No matter how much I wished for it to end, the dizziness kept going.

And then, like I'd landed safely beneath a parachute, the storm subsided.

I opened my eyes, expecting to see the guards rushing in to jab me with more needles, but instead I saw the empty side wall of the room. Then I saw another carbon copy behind it, and a third beyond that like I was looking at the frames of a movie stacked one behind the other. It was just like what'd happened the day before, only I couldn't brush it off as a panic attack this time. As I moved my head slightly to either side, the cascading images moved with me. The room carried on infinitely. My vision had narrowed to a fixed perspective, like I was looking through binoculars. I could only see down the barrel of my sight with the endless slices of scenery stretching on with nothing in my periphery.

It took a moment before I realized the room no longer held a sound, not even the heaviness of my breathing as I frantically tried to make sense of the disorienting segments of my vision. The silence had the odd effect of absorbing my fears in its vacuum, allowing me time to think through what was happening and take stock of the situation. I could still breathe. I lifted my hand to my face to prove to myself that I still had control over my body. I expected snapshots of my hand to repeat in infinite slices, but it was whole. Same for my feet. In fact, the floor seemed like it was the only surface that I couldn't see drawn out like an accordion. Everything within reach was normal—except the flurry of papers I'd knocked off the desk hovering motionless above the floor.

I could almost explain away everything else—the loss of hearing, the vision problems, the clenching, constant tension —but a floating stack of papers was something that shouldn't've been possible. I wondered for an instant if Chaos had killed me after all, and this was life after death—a still frame in a silent movie. The longer I realized I still had consciousness, though, the more I began to reason through this new reality. I took another look at the papers suspended in air, this time eyeing them with the analytic mind that had rescued me from panic situations more than once. Chaos had done something to me after all, but I wasn't dead. I held that thought like a talisman. I began to relax little by little, letting go of some of my tension. As I did, my vision shifted. The slices of the world contracted like they were going to collapse back into one. When I looked down at the papers, they started to move slightly along their path to the floor.

The sight sent my muscles flexing in tension once more, and the slices of vision returned. The papers stopped falling.

What is going on?

As the tension returned, I realized it wasn't just my arms or legs that felt taut. This strange new vision of the world seemed tied to the same feeling I had when I picked up a heavy weight or lifted myself out of a chair, only the muscle I was using wasn't part of my body. It felt like something outside of me that I could control.

I relaxed my hold over this unseen limb completely and almost like I'd woken from a trance, the sights and sounds of my isolation room came rushing back. The papers fell to the floor. I could hear myself breathing again.

I looked up at the security camera in the corner. The lens motors whirred.

The hazmat army would be back soon. If I had any hope at all of saving myself from a lifetime of being Valhalla's hostage, figuring out whether Chaos had given me one of the abilities Gemma told me about was my only focus now. I had work to do.

I needed to see just how far this new muscle of mine could go.

I grabbed one of the pieces of paper on the floor and balled it up, hoping to replicate what had happened.

As I tossed the piece of paper into the air, part of me wondered if I'd be able to flex again on command, but those fears subsided quickly as soon as I triggered my phantom muscle. The yellow haze appeared over my skin. The dizziness hit like a train. I held on through the violent transfer until the slices of vision appeared and I was back in the Silence. Seemed as good a name as any.

Just as I'd hoped, the ball of paper sat suspended in air in front of me.

This time I didn't hesitate. I reached out to grab the paper to see if I could move it somewhere else, envisioning a potential scenario where I could move a guard away from the door when they entered the room. As soon as my fingers touched the surface it was like dipping my hand in ice water. More than that, though, it felt like I had control, like I could turn the piece of paper on and off like a light. All I had to do was flip the switch.

So, I did.

The paper looked no different when I took my hand away. I don't know what I expected to happen, but I wanted *something* to happen. As strange as it was to have this new, unseen part of my body, I already had the sense that I wanted it to mean something, not just make me flash a yellow light and enter a mute world where nothing moved.

I let my body relax again, already trying to piece together my next experiment as the real world came back in a blur of light and sound. I dropped down to the floor to think, sure that I only had a few seconds of freedom left before Valhalla's guards returned to force tests on me. When I looked up to see if the camera was still watching, the balled-up piece of paper still hung in the air, blocking my view.

Impossible.

For a brief second, I wondered if maybe I was still in the Silence, but the whirr of the camera and the stale air circulating in the room told me differently. Just as I had a few seconds earlier, I reached for the piece of paper. I could hardly believe it when it felt like steel to my touch. I grabbed it, pulled it, then tried to push it out of the way. It was immovable.

Frozen in time.

I didn't have a better explanation. I flexed again, surprising myself by how much I already relished the dizziness that came with the yellow light. The Silence was starting to prove intoxicating. I could see it becoming a source of escape from the world—but I still had an experiment to finish.

As soon as the slices appeared, I reached for the piece of paper and once again felt the cold rush that came from touching the surface. I repeated the sensation of flipping the mental switch, this time turning it back *on* again. Once I took my hand away, I relaxed and waited for the real world to come back.

The crumpled wad of paper fell to the floor.

The loud mechanical whirr of the door locks deflated my moment of triumph. I stood flat-footed, at once ready to use my new power to protect myself but also too practiced at accepting I wouldn't be able to survive without help.

"Ms. Weeks wanted you fed," the man in the hazmat suit said flatly. He carried a plate of long-ago reheated beans.

While his smoker's voice rumbled like thunder in my ears, my eyes were focused on the door that drifted closed just out of reach. I wanted to run through the shrinking opening, but I'd never make it in time.

Time. Maybe I wasn't as attached to it as everyone else anymore.

My gaze turned to the locks on the door as it clicked shut. If I could somehow freeze them in place so they couldn't be re-armed, maybe I could escape once the guard left. There'd be other guards to deal with on my way out, but I also knew now that I could do something they couldn't. It was scary, in a way, to feel the rush of power that came with this new ability. I both loved the feeling and hated it. It felt like I was standing in Britt's shoes—secure in the knowledge I could control anything that got in my way.

Moral questions of power would have to wait until I got my freedom back. When the man turned to set the plate of beans down, I readied myself to flex and go for the door as soon as it opened.

The door swung wide on its hinges before the guard could turn back around. Another man stepped through, and his eyes fixed on mine at the same moment my skin flashed yellow, and the dizziness took me away.

Back in the deadened air of the Silence, the door transformed into cascading rectangles stretching as far back as my eyes could see, but the door in my little bubble of time was still within reach. When I turned my infinite gaze toward the guard, I took a nauseating step back in surprise. His eyes bore into mine, multiplied by thousands of copies watching behind him. The flash of my skin's light had painted his pupils with streaks of yellow. I wondered if he could still see while I had him frozen in place. The way he looked at me—fearful and ready to fight—was how I imagined others might feel once they knew what I could do.

The shiver I felt when I came into contact with the door was more intense than when I'd touched the paper. It was like sticking my hand in a bucket of cold electricity—the pain made me recoil. I tried again, this time placing my fingers only on the locking mechanism, which was less painful to touch but still jarring. I was just about to mentally flip the switch when I stopped to work through what was about to happen. After I touched the ball of paper, it had hung frozen in the air and somehow had a density like iron. If the same thing happened with the door lock, it would keep the door connected to it open, which meant the guards would immediately take notice. I needed them gone before I tried my escape. I turned my attention to the console controlling the locks instead. It wasn't connected to the door, and if I froze whatever machinery inside sent the signal to the lock, I could still get out without the guards knowing something was different.

A burning sensation started in my chest and began to

radiate toward my arms and legs. It already felt like I was starting to strain to stay in the Silence. I wasn't sure how long I could keep my flex going.

I moved gingerly around the nearest guard, fighting back the urge to wretch as the movement made me even dizzier. Any visions I had of running away in the paused world evaporated. The pain grew more intense with each step. After a couple of agonizing lurches, I got to the control panel. I touched my hand to the console and flipped my mental switch.

Every step back to my starting point had the dizzying feel of walking a tightrope over a canyon. I didn't know what it would be like to vomit in the Silence, but it felt like I was about to find out. I repositioned myself close to where the guard would expect me and relaxed my new muscle. Once again, the world came back in a rush of movement.

"Weird," the guard said. He shook his head.

The other guard looked over his shoulder. "What is it?"

I held my breath.

"For a second, it looked like she was glowing."

"Mark it down in the notes and get a picture of the contact point."

The man blinked through his confusion and pointed his console at my wrist, right where Chaos had clawed through my suit. The flash of the camera left a lingering spot in my eyes. "Got it."

I'd gotten lucky after all. I hid my expression behind the hair that had fallen in front of my eyes, trying not to give away my excitement to see them leave as they filed out the door. I'd never been good at poker. It felt like an hour went by before the metal door clanged shut behind them. I waited to hear the mechanical click of the locks snapping back into place, unsure of what my next move could be if my plan failed.

Seconds ticked by without the sound of the locks moving.

It had worked.

I GAVE the guards a few seconds to get down the hall before I made my break. Not that I knew where I was. Finding a way out was a problem for Future Zoe.

After a deep breath, I reached for the door without waiting for doubt to slow me down. I almost shrieked with excitement when it swung open easily. Two tiptoed steps later and I was out in the hallway—alone. My not-so-carefully-crafted plan was in motion.

I moved quietly down the empty corridor until I noticed a patch of sunlight coming through the bottom of a door at the end. There were no shadows moving inside. Any other path took me down the hallway where the guards were probably just noticing I was gone, so I gently turned the handle and slipped inside.

The room was a maze of white desks with a fire exit sign beaming overhead in the back. I'd found my exit, but in between me and the way out were dozens of Valhalla researchers and almost as many guards.

"Oh no…"

Everyone stopped to stare at me with a shared look of wide-eyed shock. I looked back with a similar frozen state of surprise.

And then the alarm sounded.

The piercing screech acted like a match to gasoline. At once, guards started running toward me from all sides. My paths of escape through the bank of confused-looking researchers dwindled with each second I let pass. I wasn't some action star. I'd never been athletic at anything. The most I'd ever done was rowing across lakes, and I didn't think my knowledge of boats would help against a bunch of muscular guards carrying neural guns.

I tried running anyway, scrambling across the nearest desk

in front of me as the guards blocked my escape on both sides. I got across two of them, pushing past the scared researcher who shrank from me like I carried the plague. I could feel the guard behind me closing in, and as I tried to cross the third desk his arm snaked around me in a headlock.

I flexed into the Silence immediately, unsure of what else to do. Back in the stillness of my void, I thought about freezing the man, but in the moment I couldn't bring myself to do it. I had no idea what the effect would be, and I couldn't risk killing him. Instead, I maneuvered my head from beneath his grasp and tried to make it back to the exit door. I could only get a few steps before the pain and nausea overwhelmed me. The sudden agony forced me to relax my hold, and the room resumed its frantic pace. The guard who'd held me saw me and cursed. The next guard rushed toward me, and I could see by the tense, fearful look on his face that he wasn't going to try to subdue me like the other. Sure enough, he reached for his neural gun and pointed the double-barreled pistol right at my head.

I entered the Silence just in time. The charge of the electric pellets sparked like a picture of fireworks at the back of the weapon. I was close enough to not have to take a step to touch the gun. I switched it off, freezing it in place, and then relaxed again on my way past him. Making the transition between the Silence and the real world while moving was almost as stomach-turning as trying to walk in my surreal world. Still, I kept going, leaving another bewildered guard behind me.

There was only one man left between me and the exit, somehow looking more scared than I was. His hand hovered over his weapon, but he hesitated, glancing between me and the mayhem behind me. I don't know where the burst of confidence came from that made me run toward him instead of the door to the stairwell. Maybe it was intuition. Whatever it was, it paid off because the guard flinched and moved back against the desk leaving me plenty of room to run by.

I bolted through the door and down the stairs, no longer as scared as I was but also nowhere near making my escape. The guards' footsteps pounded behind me. I vaulted down steps three at a time, and it still sounded like they were closing in.

The men screamed for someone to stop me. A group of people standing on a landing a few floors down looked from the guards' voice above, and then to me rushing toward them. The guards were close enough now that I could feel the steps shaking beneath me. I grabbed the railing and spun past the gawking bystanders and straight into someone else coming the other way. A guy carrying a tray of food emptied it all over me during the collision. We twisted as we fell, and the commotion must have masked the sound of the neural gun firing. The man's eyes rolled back into his head. His muscles seized. He dropped into a heap on the stairwell with the wires of the pellet still sparking electricity on his back. The people on the landing screamed.

The guard carrying the gun looked from the man to me. I held the tray out like the impotent shield it was.

He fired again.

I flexed and froze the tray in place. When I re-entered the world, the shock pellets bounced off the plastic rectangle like it was made of stone.

The guard stared at the tray in disbelief.

I took advantage of his hesitation and ran. The door at the bottom of the next set of stairs led to a breezeway across Chalk Avenue. While the guard was still yelling through his radio for the rest of the security team to come up from the lower levels, I jumped down the last couple of steps and through the door.

The guard appeared through the narrow door window. I flexed and placed my hand on the door handle. My mental switch flipped, and when I came out of the Silence, the man's inertia sent him face-first into the immovable door. He kept slamming it with his shoulder as I backed into the breezeway. I could still hear him beating his fist against the window as I ran through the exit on the other side.

Finally, I reached the lowest level and found a door to the trash recycler in the alley between our building and its neighbor. I almost collapsed in relief. Against every self-doubting bone in my body, I'd made it.

But I also had nowhere to go.

I couldn't go to my apartment; Valhalla would be sure to look for me there first. I couldn't go to the World Union; they'd be just as likely to lock me up for study as Valhalla had been. I had no money, no phone, and I was about to go running down the streets of Seattle in a patient scrub covered in mashed potatoes.

There was nothing to do but come up with a plan while I walked. If I stood in the alley, they'd be able to take me back in without anyone noticing. I cinched my gown around my waist to make it at least look like a dress and hurried into the flow of people on the sidewalk. Luckily, it must have been lunch hour. The street was packed. I only noticed a few odd looks at my get-up as I tried to walk as fast as I could without coming off like someone running from the scene of a crime.

Gemma. Every mental avenue of escape I went down kept coming back to her. Despite the fact that she worked for the people currently trying to bring me back in for study, I had a hard time seeing her give me up to the security team. That was probably naive. She did say she'd help me get out of it, though. Regardless, my options were limited, and my only hope was that she'd at least provide a buffer between me and the security teams. She brought me to Seattle to save her daughter, after all. I couldn't do that if I was locked away in a cell.

If I was going to ask for her help, I didn't have long to do it. They'd probably be monitoring Gemma's phone soon. I tried to convince myself they weren't already. I ducked into the first place that looked like it had a phone I could use—a bookstore. The poor woman behind the counter did the best she could not to react to my disheveled state. She handed me the receiver and retreated to the register to help another customer. I dialed Gemma's number.

"Hello?" Gemma's voice sounded hopeful, like she expected me to call.

"Gemma, it's—."

"Hold on."

While I sat silent on the line, I could hear Gemma's fingers tapping on a keyboard, then her footsteps walking quickly before a sharp click of a door closing in the background. "We should have a couple minutes before they realize my tap is dead. Are you okay?"

"For now. I don't want to mix you up in this but—"

"What can I do?" she asked.

I hadn't thought of what, exactly, I wanted from her. At the moment, I almost needed someone else to give me options. I was all out of plans.

"I'm not sure what to do next," I said.

"Okay. We're going to get you out of this. Do you know where the Capitol Hill Hotel is?"

I searched my shallow memory of the city and tried to piece together images from my walks. "I think so. It's between Valhalla and my apartment?"

"That's the one. Go there and register under the name Fiona Martin. I'll call ahead and set up payment. I'll meet up with you later tonight once I know they're not tailing me, and we'll figure out what to do next."

I couldn't help but let out a shuddered breath. The woman behind the counter shot a nervous look at me.

"Go on, Zoe. You need to hurry. I'll be there as soon as I can."

I left the phone lying on the counter. The door clanged behind me as I melted back into the flow of people on the street. The hotel was only a few blocks away. For the first time since Chaos sent my life spiraling, I enjoyed a moment of hope.

Or at least the thought of it.

CHAPTER SEVEN

THE CITY never felt so small until I was a fugitive walking through it. I was careful not to draw attention to myself—moving like a mouse through the shadows, terrified of being caught if I stumbled into the light. Britt was the spotlight I'd run from for a thousand miles. Now I had a whole corporation after me, one with deep pockets and a host of guards who probably wanted nothing more than to lock me back in a cell, never to be set free.

As soon as I walked into the spacious lobby of the hotel, I wanted to run back out. With a jam-packed restaurant on one side and a busy waiting room on the other, there was no place for a woman in a dirty patient scrub to hide.

The young girl working behind the counter smiled in a practiced way as I approached with arms crossed over the food stain on my chest. "Do you have a reservation?"

Many.

I panicked for a second as I tried to recall the name Gemma gave me. "It's, um, Fiona…"

Her hands stayed suspended over the keyboard while she waited for me to finish.

"Martin!" I eventually blurted out. "Sorry. Getting used to a new stage name. I'm an actress."

Just not a very good one.

The girl smiled politely as she tapped away on her screen. She reached down to grab a pair of key cards. "You're all set. Non-smoking, a beautiful view of the Seattle Bay, and two twin beds. Your wife paid already."

I nodded as if I expected the news, because apparently I really was an actress now.

Before I left, the woman told me to enjoy my visit to beautiful Seattle. It was a perfectly normal comment that felt more like a gut punch. This was supposed to be my new home, but it was becoming increasingly clear that I'd have to leave if I wanted to stay free. Maybe I was doomed to live the life of a transient now. I felt like I'd be lucky if I could even make it to another city.

It was too much to think about on top of everything else. I hurried off the elevator when the doors opened to the tenth floor and found my room at the end of an empty hallway. All I wanted to do was shut myself in, lock the door, and sleep for days. The simple act of walking in and hearing the latch click into place behind me instilled some welcome calmness. I'd bought myself a brief period of safety.

A set of sliding glass doors gave me a view of Seattle Bay, as advertised. One of the ferries inched its way into the transportation terminal dock. It punctuated its arrival with a bellowing horn.

I watched the tiny stream of people flowing off the boat ramp and thought about the power inside me now, sitting there like a muscle waiting to be used. I thought about the rest of my life and what it would look like when I could flex that muscle and do something no one else could. How it might scare others—scare me—and ignite a race to see who could control the virus. There was no scenario that ended with me happily living my days out in solitude. Every mental path I went down ended in disaster.

I decided to look for something brown and expensive in the mini fridge rather than stare out the window and mentally doomscroll the future.

A gentle knock on the door interrupted my search.

"Fiona?" a whispered voice said from the other side of the door.

Well, she got here fast. I flipped on the videocomm beside the door to make sure it was Gemma. My breath caught as the image appeared.

No. NO!

Britt stood in the hallway, looking into the camera with a slanted grin. I didn't want to believe it. The part of me that had hoped she was out of my life forever crumbled. I wanted to run, but there was nowhere else to go, nothing I could freeze in time to keep her from finding me again and again.

"Get *out of here*!" I yelled into the speaker, lashing out in the only way I could.

"Honey, please, keep your voice down. Don't make a scene."

I slammed my palm against the button to turn the comm off and backed away from the door. My misophonia swelled to life. The sound of the ferry screeching its horn again was like a knife buried in my chest that I couldn't rip out.

Her muffled voice came through the cracks. "Listen, Zo. I get it. I'm not the person you want to see right now."

"You don't *get* anything. It's not just right now. I never want to see you again." I hadn't fought back against her in so long, the words were like a foreign language I had yet to master.

"You don't mean that."

"I mean every word."

There was a long enough pause that I thought for a second she might've walked away. I turned the videocomm screen on again and stuck my thumb over the camera on my side to make sure she couldn't see me. Britt was still there, standing with her hands in the back pockets of her jeans. As tall as she was, she barely fit on the screen. She started to play aimlessly with the long braid draping over her left shoulder. It was how I always used to wear my hair before she started doing it. Her nails were ragged. She'd been chewing them again. Her eyes were red and puffy like she'd been crying recently.

What do I care?

"Zo," she said. She was the only person who ever called me that. "I've been… I've really been worried."

"Don't be."

She waited for another guest to walk past before talking again. "When I woke up that morning and you were gone, I called everybody—the police, Social Services, your job. I was frantic. No one knew anything."

I said a silent *thank you* to my old lab supervisor for not giving up my secret.

"It's funny," she said, brightening for a moment despite having to wipe away a tear. "I knew exactly why you left before I even knew for sure you were gone. I should've apologized sooner."

A sudden wave of curiosity drowned out my resolve to stay silent. In our four years together, I couldn't remember her ever apologizing once. She considered it losing, and Britt hated to lose.

"What are you sorry for?" I asked.

"I'm sorry for how I acted."

A vague attempt. I pressed my thumb harder on the camera. "That's not an apology."

"I know, I know. I'm not good at this." She placed her hands on her hips and spoke in a lower voice so only I could hear her. "I was overbearing."

I waited. "And?"

"And I was selfish. And I wasn't trusting of you."

Overbearing and selfish were easy concessions. It was the admission of not trusting that made me almost take my thumb off the camera. What gave me pause was the subtle change in her eyes—a victorious glint that said she understood the effect her words were having.

Her green eyes, bright as a spring leaf. They made her different, marked her as special. It's what had attracted me when we first met.

"You're not wearing your glasses," I said.

She gave a thin smile. "I don't have you around to remind me."

I could feel the familiar tidal pull of her charm, the one that would eventually recede, leaving me with the woman who doled out abuse like it was her only means of showing attention. "How did you find me?" I asked.

"Oh, it wasn't too hard," she replied. It was exactly like her to say something seemingly innocent that was a clear warning beneath its thin veneer—She'd found me once and she could do it again. "I just needed to know why you left."

"I left the way I did because I don't want to see you anymore," I said, refocusing. "That's forever. We're done, Britt. There's no going back."

"You can't be serious. Think of all I've done for you. All I've sacrificed so you could have your precious *career*. I know I've screwed up, but I haven't done anything to warrant this. I don't deserve it."

"And what do I deserve? To be hit again?"

"No," she said, her voice losing its edge. "That wasn't me and you know it. I'm not that person."

"I know exactly who you are."

Her shoulders slumped. For the first time I could remember, she looked resigned. "So, you're serious."

"Yes."

I wondered what filled her head in the pause that followed.

Her expression was blank, giving no clues as to whether she wanted to walk away in silence or come through the door and bash my skull in.

She can't anymore. Whatever Chaos had done to me, the one thing I was sure about was that I was different now. Maybe that's why I felt so sure of myself when telling her no this time, something I'd hardly had the strength to do before. It was a strange sense of confidence and control. I held it like a sword made just for my hands.

"Zoe?" she said.

"What?"

"Before I go, I just want to say one thing."

"What is it?"

She reached into her pocket to grab a key card with my room number emblazoned on the side. "You should really complain about the security in this place."

I was too surprised to react. Britt came barreling into the room, knocking me off balance. One foot caught another, and I stumbled backward, hitting the back of my head against the wall. My ears rang instantly. A dark curtain formed around the edge of my vision, moving like an eclipse over my sight.

"Don't worry, Zo. I'm not gonna hurt you." The words were like a distant echo. "You're not worth the jail time."

I felt her forearm across my throat. She used her weight to pin me to the wall.

"I just want to know who you were fucking that brought you here, that's all. Was it Jackie? Ben? All I want is a name. Who took you from me?"

"Nobody…" I said. Little by little, the veil of darkness started to lift.

"Nobody? You don't register under a false name in a hotel if you're meeting *nobody*."

"…Gemma."

The name was out of my mouth before I could think to stop it. As my vision returned, the inferno building behind

Britt's eyes came into focus. Whatever control she'd shown so far had reached its end.

"Gemma? Who is *Gemma*?!"

Her forearm pressed harder against my throat, cutting off the circulation in my neck. I swatted at her and tried to slide away, but she was too strong. She was always too strong.

I only had a few seconds of consciousness left. I flexed the only muscle I had that was more powerful than hers.

My skin started to glow.

The pain and the panic of having the life choked out of me followed me into the Silence. I was still pinned against the wall. I still couldn't breathe. With the world standing still, I fought to get air. I pulled myself down the slight angle of her arm until I was finally able to free myself. The skin on my neck burned raw. I slipped away from Britt's rigid arm now hovering above an empty wall.

Standing there in the vacuum created by my power, I clutched at my bruised throat and stared at the stacked vertical images of Britt stretching to infinity. I studied her eyes while I recovered. They held a glimmer of light like she'd been frozen in time by the flash of a camera bulb. That glimmer helped me regain my strength more than anything else. It was a reminder of what I could do.

My job was only half done. I could get away from her in the Silence, but as soon as I let it go, she'd be right back at my throat, and maybe next time I wouldn't have a chance to use the tool Chaos had given me. I needed something to freeze, something that would keep her where she was.

What if I froze her?

I had no idea what would happen. Would she be able to breathe? Could I kill her if I left her frozen too long? As much as I wanted to be free of Britt, I couldn't go to prison or back to Valhalla and give up my freedom to do it. *Not that I'm free now.* I also considered the biting cold feeling I had when I flipped my switch on the piece of paper and the neural gun.

Those were barely larger than my hand. If I tried it on something as big as Britt, it might kill me.

There had to be another way.

I grimaced through the vertigo of walking around her. I considered her clothes, her boots—even the braid dangling off her shoulder. My hold over my flex grew weaker with each second my decision paralysis stretched on. The glow on my skin already looked faint. Everything seemed intimidating to try until I knew for sure what my limits were. *Even frozen, she's getting in my head.*

I circled around to the arm that had pinned me to the wall, fighting the overwhelming urge to empty my guts. Hanging from a chain on her neck was the ring she'd bought herself as part of our "marriage pact." She'd asked me to marry her several times, and I always told her I wasn't ready yet, so she bought two rings instead to act as a promise between us. Mine was a hideous tangle of silver bands with emerald stones that were supposed to be leaves. I never wore it. Hers was a single wide platinum band. She wore it around her neck saying she'd save it there for the day I finally gave in.

I keyed in on the dull metal as my grasp on the Silence waned. I placed my fingers around the ring and instantly felt the rush of ice through my body. Flipping the switch to stop it in time, I took my fingers off the metal and stood back, trying to decide what I was going to do once I relaxed my hold on the Silence and returned to the world.

Part of me wanted to stay in the room and watch her struggle to get free. I wanted so badly to see Britt looking scared for once, to feel the same way I had so many times over the years—helpless and stuck. I wanted her to know things had changed. She couldn't control me like she used to, not with my new power. The images were almost too good to miss.

But I had to.

I looked over my shoulder at the repeating images of the hallway. The door was too far for me to make it after holding the flex for as long as I already had, but if I ran as soon as I relaxed my hold on the Silence, that would be enough to give me the head start I needed.

Just in case.

I started walking toward the hallway. Each step brought a fresh wave of nausea, each more intense than the last. By the time I made it to the door, I could barely stand. My head swirled, struggling to focus. The feeling of wanting to turn my insides out couldn't be eased. My body kept telling me I had a poison inside it needed to be rid of, but I couldn't carry through with getting it out. I even tried to vomit. It only made the pain in my gut double.

By the fifth step, I had to stop. The pain didn't. I took a couple of steps back until it was manageable again. The urge to relax my strained grip on the Silence was overwhelming. A few feet of safety would have to do.

Here we go.

I relaxed my mental muscle and held on through the disorienting ride back to reality. If all else failed and she somehow managed to come after me, I could move away and try to flex again to create distance between us. At least I hoped I could. I was banking on the power of adrenaline to push me through if my new muscle decided to fail me.

"Tell me!" Britt screamed as her forearm thrust forward into the now empty wall in front of her. She looked around, her face contorted in confusion. Her eyes found mine, and I realized I'd forgotten to run.

Britt lunged.

As soon as she turned her head, she was horse-collared, betrayed by momentum and a necklace frozen in time. I stopped my escape long enough to hear her struggling to breathe after smashing her throat into the necklace. She hung from the piece of jewelry like a witch on the gallows, grasping at the chain holding her in place. Eventually she pulled herself back up to standing. Her chest heaved. Her eyes were wild with anger. The skin on her face flushed red.

And then Britt's flailing paused abruptly. She glared over my shoulder. "Who the fuck are you?"

The crack of gunfire filled the narrow hallway, followed by a sound like lightning cutting through the air.

Gemma stood behind me holding a neural gun. I looked back at Britt. Her body collapsed as her eyes rolled back into her head. Her tongue blocked the gurgling sound in her throat. She was choking as she hung from the frozen necklace.

I ran over to her and hoisted her up until her head bobbed forward, dislodging her tongue. Gemma followed me inside and shut the door.

"Is she going to die?" I asked.

"This is the woman you told me about? If I had my way she would. But no—she'll wake up in a few hours with a bad headache."

If she thought it was strange for a necklace to hover in mid-air, Gemma didn't show it.

"WU Security's on their way," she said.

"No!" I said too forcibly. I didn't want to deal with the World Union finding out about me on top of everything else. "We can't."

"Zoe, don't worry. There's no chance she'll wake up."

I looked to the necklace. "I wasn't talking about that."

Gemma followed my stare and then nodded. "Can you undo it?"

I hesitated, unsure of what I should tell her about the changes Chaos had caused.

"It's okay," she said. "I saw what you're capable of. I managed to get a hold of the recordings from Valhalla. Go ahead. I'll hold her."

Gemma stepped forward and took Britt's weight. She watched me, waiting with no small hint of eagerness behind her eyes.

I'm already a sideshow.

I imagined the Security team would be at our door soon. Without thinking too much more, I flexed and entered the Silence. I barely noticed the chill in my fingers this time when I switched the necklace back on.

When I came back, Gemma stumbled backwards under the sudden collapse of Britt's body, barely catching herself against the wall. She let my ex's limp form slip to the floor.

"You and I have a lot to talk about," Gemma said, panting.

Tell me about it.

We both turned our heads at the knock on the door. "Security!" a man bellowed.

"Get in the closet," Gemma whispered, "and don't say a word. Let me handle this."

There was no time to argue. I jumped into the walk-in and peaked through the slats in the door to watch what happened. Gemma made a show of running to the door and flung it open. Her movements were frantic, and her voice cracked as she thanked the Security detail for coming so quickly. It was the staged monologue of an actress who knew her audience well. The guards ate it up, puffing at the chest as they surveyed Britt's unconscious body at their feet.

"Neural guns are not to be used lightly," the officer said.

"I'm sorry, officer. My husband insisted I carry one. He bought it for me."

I should've been amazed at her improv, but Gemma had proven to be full of surprises.

"What will you do with her?" she asked.

"She'll need a doctor. We can drive her by the hospital first."

Gemma hugged her arms to her chest. "She's so dangerous, I worry for those poor nurses. I just wish there was another option."

"We could take her to the station," the other officer said. "One of the EMTs can watch after her."

She placed a hand on his shoulder. "Thank you. That would be a huge stress relief."

"As for the victim," the first man said. "We'll need to speak to them."

"Of course, of course. I was so panicked, I told her to run to another hotel. I don't know which one she went to yet, but as soon as she contacts me, I'll have her call you immediately."

It was a masterful performance. In only a few minutes, she'd had the officers believing it was their idea to take Britt to a holding cell to recover and managed to deflect questions about me.

After one last promise to have me call their office for a statement, Gemma showed the officers out. I opened the closet door. Gemma let out a rush of air like she was stepping out of someone's skin and breathing again for the first time.

"Well," she said. "Still got those community theater chops."

So much had happened since I saw her at the hospital, I felt like it was all about to come flooding out of my mouth at once. I was so overwhelmed.

"We still need to talk," Gemma said, "but that can wait." She wrapped her arms around me in a hug. "Let's get you somewhere safe first. I know just the place."

CHAPTER EIGHT

I'D BEEN to therapy enough times to recognize the tactic of letting an awkward silence force a conversation. Gemma waited with a patient, content smile as we traveled east with the skyline of Seattle behind us. Maybe it wouldn't be so bad talking about everything once we were at this supposed safe house. Until then, I tried to think of a way to signal I wasn't ready yet without resorting to a lame chat about the weather.

"Your truck is pretty nice." My voice rose at the end, making it sound like a question.

Nailed it.

Gemma nodded as if she took the hint anyway. She tapped her finger on the leather-bound wheel. "Valhalla sprang for it when I told them I had a better offer down in Los Angeles. They hate losing talent, especially to a company like Abica."

"That's the place run by AI?"

"Synthetic human—calls herself Mira. I met her once. Too intimidating to work for."

"I have a hard time imagining you as intimidated."

She laughed. "Maybe *too much of an overbearing witch* is a

better way to put it. Anyway, Valhalla didn't want to let me go, and I'm not above taking bribes. I especially like the seats."

The whole inside of the luxury sport truck felt like it was meant for people who had a favorite brand of caviar. My jeans, t-shirt, and jacket seemed like an insult, in comparison. I should've packed a nice black dress for my latest attempt at a disappearing act.

As a silent pause settled in again, the scenes of Britt's attack rumbled beneath the surface of my fragile calm. I saw her face appear on the videocomm screen again, then the blazing hatred in her eyes when she held me against the wall. My throat tightened. The random jingling of Gemma's keychain started to stab at my ears with increasing volume. I dug through my pocket for my headphones like a junkie looking for a fix. Just putting my fingers on the earbud case let me breathe. I wedged the earbuds in and held a breath long enough so that the building tension could leave my body along with my exhale.

Gemma's voice pierced the shield of white noise not long after.

"Sorry." I took out an earbud. "Force of habit."

"Was I boring you?"

"No, no. I just have an anxiety thing. These help."

As nice as Gemma was, she couldn't hide the undercurrent of annoyance in her voice. "I said we're getting close. Next exit is us."

I wanted to apologize again, and then maybe again. I still hadn't convinced myself that a single negative emotion toward me wasn't going to end in disaster.

The exit could've gone unnoticed were it not for the aging green sign just before a thin, one-lane road. Only a few patches of sunlight made it through the canopy as we exited the mountain pass. A wave of déjà vu hit. The pine smell was like a time machine.

"This looks like where my folks used to live," I said.

"Oh? You haven't talked about them much."

"They live on the east coast, just outside of Tidewater. Our old house used to be in the mountains west of there, near the Asheville borough."

"Pretty country. Do you get along?"

That was almost as loaded a question as *What happened in that hotel room back there?* but she'd held off on asking me that one.

"You don't have to tell me," she added. "I know it's personal."

"No, it's okay. It's not like you and I are strangers anymore."

Gemma smiled.

"We didn't end on good terms when I left with Britt a few years ago. Turns out they were right about everything with her —they always hated Britt. They said they hoped I'd come to my senses one day, '*If she lets you*,' my mom added, which made no sense at the time."

But it made perfect sense now.

"Well, parents can't always be counted on to make the right choices in the moment. Trust me."

"Seems like Amaryn is lucky to have you, though."

It must've been the wrong thing to say, judging by the wilting smile on Gemma's face, even though every word of it was sincere. Gemma seemed like an incredible mother, especially in the face of a situation as bad as Amaryn's.

"We do the best we can," she said.

Her colorless voice laid out the words like bricks in a wall —that was the end of that line of questioning.

"Hey, look at that," she said, brightening. "The Johnson boys actually got that gas pump of theirs working." She waved to an older man pumping gas into a car that looked almost as ancient as he was.

"Hope you didn't have to pee," she said as we drove past. "That's the last bathroom until we get to the cabin, but between you and me, you don't want to see the inside of that one. Smells like it hasn't been cleaned since gas cars were actually a thing."

I laughed, if only out of relief. It was the most natural the conversation had felt since the awkward drive began. I was happy to have the Gemma I recognized back.

Before long, we were deep into a network of narrow country roads, each one purposefully anonymous, probably to keep city-dwellers from getting too comfortable. Gemma had to get out of the car on the final turn so she could open a rusty gate.

"Whatever you do, don't pull out your phone to take a picture when you see it," she said as she hopped back in the driver's seat. "Trust me. Just take it in."

"See what?"

She smiled and drove through the gate. The road wound through a dense forest of firs. Soon, the trees gave way to a clearing below.

I couldn't help my gasp. "This doesn't look real."

I'd never seen water like it before. Gemma's cabin sat on the border of a glacial lake surrounded by stony beach on one side and green fields dotted with wildflowers on the other. The tip of a glacier wound its way through mountain peaks, ending in a pool of turquoise water so clear I could see remnants of trees at the bottom, felled by storms and claimed by the lake over the years. The water emptied down a pair of angled falls close to the road.

"What do you think?" Gemma asked.

It was a scene most landscape painters would spend a lifetime trying to find. "Is it too late for me to be adopted?"

Gemma parked the car in a wide patch of dirt near the front porch. I half expected a perfectly groomed hunting dog to greet us.

"You'll be safe out here, Zoe."

She left to open the cabin, leaving me in the truck. I felt an instant surge of panic at the thought of being alone again, but the moment I got out and felt the breeze coming off the water, some of that subsided. The cool wind had a bite to it as if it carried a reminder that winter wasn't too far away. It was also a reminder that I was far, far from the sights and sounds of the city. The promise of seclusion felt real.

Gemma came out of the cabin checking her phone. "Wireless still works," she said. "Come on in. I'll give you the grand tour."

The cabin had a hand-made charm to it, like it was built by settlers and handed down through generations. Picture frames tiled the walls of the entry, each one a group shot of families set against the surrounding fields. The floorboards creaked as we walked. It sounded like the mutterings of an old ship rocking on the sea.

Gemma bypassed the living room lamps in favor of lighting a few of the candles along the fireplace mantle. "Before we get started, I wanted to be honest with you about something."

"What is it?" Honesty meant something bad was coming. No one ever prefaced good news with a warning of honesty.

"You may want to plan on staying here a while," she said. "At least for a few weeks or so. I talked to my friend in the Seattle Security office, and he said Britt would be kept in jail for a couple days, but that she'd eventually need to be released for trial."

And when she is, I've got another fight on my hands.

"But that's nothing to worry about for now," Gemma said, perhaps sensing the cloud that had come over me. "You and I can plan your transfer to another city-state before she ever sees the light of day again."

"Transfer? Last I checked, Valhalla didn't seem interested in keeping me as an employee."

"You let me handle that. I was on the verge of getting you out before you escaped, and I can always play the Abica card again if the board doesn't like it. And don't worry. You'll still be working on Chaos, but if I pull the right strings, you don't have to do it in Seattle. We've got satellite offices all over the world. Hells, maybe Amaryn and I will come too. Nothing says we have to stay here to treat her."

It was all too much to process at once, and the idea of Gemma uprooting herself and Amaryn just for me was wrong on more levels than I could count. I struggled for a response. "Thank you. I don't know what to say. I'm not sure I can make that kind of change again so soon, though."

Besides, Britt will find me no matter where I run.

"Well, like I said, we have plenty of time to figure it out. Now, let's take that tour. Your room is just down the hall."

She took my hand to lead me. I didn't want to be touched, but I couldn't come up with a nice way to say it, so she walked me down the hall like a little girl on her first day of school.

"What's this?" I asked as we passed a door that looked like it was made for a child. I took the opportunity to get my hand back. The door was barely visible, faced with the same wooden slat siding as the rest of the hallway.

"Mom's old fishing closet. She and I used to fish up here all the time in the summers when I was a kid. She kept the rods in there during the off-season, but for the life of me, I can't seem to find the key now. It's on my list of things to do when Amaryn gets better."

When. She still had hope. I admired that about Gemma, but it also felt sad to me, like I was watching her die a slow death, too.

Gemma showed me to my room, a solitary square at the end of the hallway, just down from the lone bathroom in the place. A four-poster bed filled most of it, but there was also a rolltop desk beneath a window, facing the lake. I wasn't a writer, but I could see myself starting if I had that view waiting for me each day. Gemma turned the overhead fan on. The rusted motor whined louder as it picked up speed. My ears were in no mood. It was like standing in a well filling up with screeching rats.

She put her hand on my arm to stop me from getting my earbuds in. "Before you do that, I figured we should talk." She sat on the bed and patted the white crocheted blanket beside her.

I flipped the fan off before I sat down. The wails of the motor came to a relieving end. "Sorry. Just a bit chilly."

She looked at the switch briefly. "Now that we're here, I was hoping we could talk about what happened back at Valhalla."

I still wasn't ready, but she had a right to know. Gemma was putting her neck on the line for me. The least I could do was tell her what happened.

"And just remember," she said, "You're safe out here. Valhalla isn't listening. In fact, they think you're on your way back to La Grange."

It didn't exactly fill me with comfort that she had to specify they weren't listening here. Were they listening at my apartment? Even thinking it made me worry I was adding *acute paranoia* to my stack of problems, so I buried the question for later and asked instead, "Why would they think I'm headed to La Grange?"

"I may have"—she teetered her hand—"*misguided* them a bit as to your current whereabouts."

"And they just believed you?"

"Well, according to a purchase I made for you that's arriving in La Grange tomorrow, the evidence is there. Valhalla is very protective of our assets, and that includes employees. Part of that stack of legal work you signed on day one had to do with allowing us to track your debit card use— just in case you decided to go have lunch at a competitor's dining hall. I made the purchase with the number we had on file. I'm sure you understand."

I didn't. It was an unforgivable invasion of privacy no matter how far down it was buried in paperwork.

"Anyway," she said, continuing on before I had a chance to argue. "You were about to tell me what happened."

I tucked the topic of privacy versus security away for another day. "You must've seen some of it on the recordings."

She nodded.

"So, you saw the leak happen."

"And I saw how it infected you."

A chill ran through my body as I remembered the cloud of Chaos reaching toward my face like an arm. "I started feeling different once they put me in the holding room."

"Different, how?"

"Like I had a new muscle I could control," I replied. "When I use it, that's what it feels like—flexing a muscle."

Gemma absorbed every word like a sponge. "What happens after you flex?"

"I get dizzy, nauseous—then it's like the world around me stops. There's no sound. I can't even hear myself move. I call it the Silence."

"No need for drowning out conversation with those then," she said, pointing to the earbuds in my pocket.

I couldn't tell if she was throwing a dig at me or not. "Earbuds are a little less scary than the Silence. But I'm getting used to it. It feels like a bubble in some ways. When I'm in the bubble, my vision changes."

"So, you see things?"

"No, not like that. Everything looks like an endless cascade of mirror images."

She accepted the answer with a single nod. "Okay, what else?" I had an unwelcome sense she wanted to fast-forward to the part where I had some use to her.

"Everything around me stops in time, like I'm hitting a pause button. When I touch things in the Silence, I can freeze them. Not like a temperature freeze, but more of a—"

"Like you're leaving them in the past," she said. She wasn't paying attention to me anymore. Her thoughts drifted off. I could almost see her working things out in her head. "So back in the hotel…"

"I took Britt's necklace and froze it so she couldn't move."

"Amazing. How long does it last?"

It was a question I hadn't had time to answer yet. I think the only people who knew were the guards still cleaning up my mess from the escape. "I'm not sure. I haven't left anything frozen for too long, yet."

"Can you freeze more things than one?"

"Maybe? I haven't tried."

"By taking them out of the present, do you think that makes them indestructible?"

All I could do was shrug. "With everything that's gone on, I haven't really had a chance to stop and study what happened to me."

She nodded again as if she continued to work out the tangled kinks of my situation. "We'll need to run some experiments on our own then."

"Out here?"

"Well, I'm not letting you near Seattle again in the near future." She hopped off the bed and crossed over to the dresser. She grabbed the flower vase filled with fake rose stems from on top. "This was my mother's, given to her by my grandmother. It's something I plan on giving to Amaryn someday."

"It's beautiful."

"It is. Do me a favor and don't let it break, okay?"

"What?"

Gemma let go of the vase.

Visions of shattered pieces of precious heirloom littering the wood floor spurned me to action. I flexed without even thinking. The rush of nausea ended in the Silence. I let out a relieved breath as the vase hung safely in mid-air. As I was getting used to, the shine from my skin lit the pupils of her eyes, but it was the sheer excitement behind them that registered with me. She was the personification of the drug-like rush of discovery. There was no better feeling in the world than seeing something for the first time that few others had ever witnessed. It almost made me want to put on a show for her—stopping and starting time again while moving around the room—but I still couldn't shake the feeling that I was now a freak show, and she was the carnival hawker.

I touched the vase to freeze it. I let go of my hold on the Silence and came back with my hands cupped beneath the vase just in case my powers decided to take a day off.

The vase held still, frozen along its trip toward Shattertown.

Gemma jumped when I reappeared and took a step back before transitioning to an excited laugh. Seeing it happen seemed to have taken her back in time. "This is incredible. *Incredible*. Zoe, you're... Do you have any idea how awesome this power is?"

"I do." It was a knee-jerk response. In fact, I felt like a toddler sitting behind the wheel of a race car.

"The transition was something else. Have you seen yourself? What am I saying, of course you haven't." She knelt next to the frozen vase. She touched the side of it, gingerly at first and then with more force. The vase never budged. "Power over time..."

I felt uncomfortable at the thought. "Power over vases at least."

Gemma spent a few more seconds poking and prodding the ceramic before she stood up and put her hands on her hips. "Be right back," she said before exiting the room. Rustling sounds reverberated down the narrow hallway until she came back into the room holding a hammer.

I held out a hand. "Oh gods, that's really not a good idea."

"It's science, Zoe," she proclaimed, and then swung the

hammer toward the edge of the vase with enough force to splinter it into a thousand pieces. I gasped, not just from the impact, but also because the impact had no effect on the vase at all. The hammer bounced off the fragile piece of china like she'd hit the side of a building.

I leaned in to inspect the side of the vase where she'd hit. It was perfectly smooth. "You trust my power way more than I do."

"Incredible," she repeated. Finally, she acknowledged my presence in the room again. "Oh, this vase isn't worth the paper flowers inside it. I may have embellished that part a bit. I knew you'd be too nice to let it break."

I smiled despite the realization that she'd manipulated me on a whim. *Don't be ridiculous*, I chided myself. I was only a few weeks into my recovery after being controlled for years. Sometimes it was easy to over-compensate.

"Let's try to freeze two things!" she said.

With a curiosity matching her own now, I chose the next object, taking the hammer from her hand. I tossed it in the air end over end and flexed as it started to drift past the vase. Back in the Silence, I held my breath through the nausea of kneeling down onto the floor, where the hammer sat suspended just a few inches from impact. I touched the wooden handle and felt the now-familiar flip of the switch, freezing it in place.

After my rush back to the room, I started my victory smile too early. The vase shattered against the floor, filling the hardwood beneath the hovering hammer with tiny bits of white shards and paper flower petals.

"Oh. I'm sorry, I really thought that would work."

Gemma guided me away from the minefield of debris and stood at my shoulder as we surveyed the results of our test. "Well, now we know," she said. "I'll grab a broom from the closet."

While she rummaged through the bedroom closet, I re-entered the Silence to unfreeze the hammer. I set it on the dresser before I could do more damage.

Gemma took out a small broom and dustpan. She beamed at me. "This is so exciting!"

"Is it?" I asked. "It doesn't feel like it, yet."

"It's scary, I'm sure," she said, momentarily adopting a look of concern. The excitement couldn't be contained for long. "But I think you'll see the potential soon. Oh, this is so great. With any luck, you can help cure Amaryn."

The excitement in her eyes, so contagious before, now felt as useless as her banging the hammer on the frozen vase. "I wish I could cure her, but I don't know how I'd be much help."

She looked me up and down with a smile as though she waited for the punchline. "What do you mean?"

"I mean Amaryn has a serious health issue that stopping time may not fix. I don't see how I can fix anything."

"Maybe… Maybe there's an area of her nervous system you could freeze to bring her out of the coma. Or maybe you could stop the flow of blood to whatever's killing her."

"I'm not even sure how long it would last if I could do anything." I looked down at the shattered pieces of the vase. "I'd probably make it worse."

"You don't know that."

"I have a pretty good history."

"You could try, at least," she said, her face darkening. "After all I've done for you, you could try."

I looked at her in silence, suddenly unrecognizable in her seething calm, like a crone losing the grasp of her glamour. This was the same woman who saved me, I told myself. I needed to remember. The person who held the broom at her side like she might break it over my head any second couldn't be a monster in waiting. This wasn't Gemma.

After a few seconds, her storm passed. She blinked as she

came through it. "I'm sorry," she said. "Of course, you shouldn't do anything you're not comfortable with."

"No, it's okay. Maybe I could think about ways I could help."

Gemma shook her head. "Don't be silly. You're under enough stress as it is. I can't imagine."

"I'll survive."

She smiled as I said the words with a practiced look of mother's pride. I was almost equally as proud of myself. That kind of positive confidence felt like wearing someone else's clothes.

But they were clothes that seemed to fit.

"I'm gonna go make us some tea," she said. "You okay in here?"

I nodded.

Gemma hesitated, then reached out to push a strand of hair out of my face. "You're going to change the world, Zoe Daniel." She stepped back and handed me the broom. "Right after you clean this up."

CHAPTER NINE

THE NEXT MORNING, I woke up to an empty cabin. I stumbled through the fog of morning brain, hoping once again that the last few days would prove to be some sort of elaborate nightmare. The mental tendons connecting me to the Silence were still there, though. I could feel them under my control. *Maybe tomorrow.* I shifted onto my side until I could see the mountains through the sheer curtains. At least I had a nice view of the Cascades while I settled back into the acceptance of my unwelcome reality.

The smell of coffee drifted in from the kitchen. Gemma said she'd make some before she left, despite me telling her my plan was to sleep until Winter's Day. She wanted to head back to Seattle early to settle things with Amaryn's doctors, who'd offered a tentative plan to keep her on life support for another week or two. She also wanted to stop by Valhalla to make sure my tracks were well-covered. The quicker she could return things to semi-normal at the lab, the better chance I had to hide at the cabin for as long as I needed to figure things out. Not that Valhalla would ever stop looking for me. *Add another stalker to my list.* But, as long as Gemma got the heat turned down some, it gave me a chance.

A chance to do what, though?

The answer would have to wait. Making life decisions was too grown-up a task for so early in the morning. Instead, I closed my eyes to listen to the sounds of the meadow, relishing the calm of the wilderness for as long as I could until thoughts of Britt interrupted. Her return felt like a betrayal of hope. I wouldn't make that mistake again. Despite Gemma's claim that Britt would eventually be on her way to prison for a long time, I couldn't let my guard down until I heard her cell door shut. At least I wouldn't have to testify against her in court. WU victim laws granted me a private deposition with the judge and lawyers. I'd never have to see Britt again if that's what I wanted.

Wanted wasn't a strong enough word. I craved a life without fear of her.

I drifted in and out of naps until after lunch, then spent the rest of the day playing "Valhalla Cops or a Stiff Breeze?" every time nature had the audacity to make a noise. I finally relaxed enough to eat something around sundown. One sandwich and four beers later and my mind was blissfully quiet.

I woke up the next morning on the couch—still not in a nightmare, still without a plan. If I was going to run again, I had to pick a direction. With Gemma gone until after dinner and no TV to watch trashy shows, that left me another day to kill, and I was determined not to spend it picturing every path that could go wrong.

I decided to go on a hike while I waited for her to get back. I'd always done my best decision-making by distracting my brain with something else while it processed. So, rather than figuring out my next destination, I chose to concentrate on the changes Chaos had caused in me instead. I was my own human trial now, no government approval needed. It made working on solving the virus's mystery convenient.

It wasn't technically correct to call Chaos a virus, but it

was the closest thing I could think of to describe how it took over cells. As I traced the edge of the lake on my way to the trail, I thought back to the moment when I first felt Chaos's effects, after I drew my first syringe of it. I thought I was having a panic attack at the time. Now I understood that the frames of time splitting my vision were the first symptoms of Chaos's infection, but what I didn't understand was why it didn't fully take me over then. It's like it was testing me, and once it knew it could spread, it bided its time until it could fully infect me. How the virus traveled through what should have been an impenetrable hazmat suit was one of the dozen puzzles I impatiently wanted to solve. I passed the trailhead at the base of the waterfall and started up, already lamenting the fact that isolation meant I had no tools for research.

I'll talk to Gemma about it tonight. Maybe she can sneak an electron microscope or two from the lab. In the meantime, I wanted to see how far I could push my limits. If my abilities were a new muscle, maybe I could strengthen them like one.

Since nothing moved in the Silence except me, my phone timer wasn't going to be much help. I had to resort to a mental stopwatch for my first test. I stopped and sat down on a fallen log. I wanted to see how long I could stay in one place while in the Silence before I was forced to come back. I took a deep breath and held it through the rush of nausea. The Silence divided my view of the trees into cascading rectangles. Like a kid learning how time works, I repeated the word in my head as I counted—*one rectangle, two rectangle.* The first tinge of strain started when I got to ten. By fifteen, it felt like I was sweating. I finally let go just as I hit twenty. Even though my abilities weren't a real muscle, I came back gasping for air as if I'd just bench pressed a mule.

After taking a minute to rest, I wanted to try again. Twenty seconds. My latent competitive side, not seen since swim team, started to get angry that I couldn't get past it. On the third attempt, I managed to eke it out to twenty-one and came back smiling through my labored breaths. The repetition zapped my strength, but I couldn't help but keep the momentum going. I was halfway to a runner's high, and I hadn't gotten off the log yet.

I eyed the path ahead of me for my next test. It switched back to the right about fifty yards ahead on its way up the mountain. I wondered if I could get to the bend in under twenty seconds before I lost my grip on the Silence. I got up, dusted the moss off my pants, and got ready. After drawing a line in the dirt with my shoe to mark my start, I flexed. I waited to take my first step until the sounds of the forest muted.

Every movement, every swing of my leg brought with it another layer of nausea and pain radiating down the center of my body. I felt like a burrito left in the microwave too long. I tried psyching myself up by pretending the next step would lead me out of the storm. I only managed about five big strides before my legs felt like they might snap if I pushed them another inch. I relaxed, unknotting my muscle. It was the first time I'd ever come back from the Silence in the middle of that kind of pain, and it lingered for a moment like a cramp untangling itself.

I looked back at the line I'd drawn in the dirt.

There were no footsteps in between.

I stared at the patch of trail waiting for my eyes to stop playing tricks on me. I told myself I needed to get used to the fact that I could do things that should have been impossible. I had to start thinking of myself as different, because I was.

I logged the unexpected data point in my phone's note-taking app and added a new line for my next test. I re-entered the Silence. Instead of seeing how far I could move at once this time, I took a step and stopped. The initial wave of pain plateaued. I took another step. The pain intensified, ramping up even though I was resting in between. I had hoped the pauses would reset the sensation of nerves being electrified. *So much for that theory.* I managed another two grueling steps before my bones threatened to snap in two. I backtracked to roughly where I started and waited for the pain to recede. When I started forward again, I took smaller strides. The pain built up to the same intensity no matter how short I made my steps along the way. I made it to roughly the same spot before I relented, riding through the wave of nausea as I returned to the sounds of the forest.

As I waited for the remnants of soreness to subside, I held my eyes closed and assessed what I'd learned. It wasn't about how many steps I took; it was about how far away from my point of entry I was. I imagined it like a rubber band around my waist that became harder to stretch the more I tried to lengthen it.

A rubber band might stretch, but it recovered as soon as you let the tension off. I'd seen that already. If I left the Silence and immediately flexed again to go back in, then kept going, how far could I get? I pictured it like walking through time— which is a phrase I would've committed myself for if I'd uttered it a year ago—but it made sense now.

I drew another line in the dirt with my foot and blew out a few deep breaths.

When I entered the Silence and hit the limit of my distance, I let my muscle relax and then immediately flexed it again. I repeated the number of steps, only this time I could barely make it to five. Every time I relaxed and flexed back in, I couldn't make it as far as I had the previous time. It was like repeatedly folding a piece of paper in half until it was nearly impossible after only a few folds. By the fifth segment of my time walk, I had to stop. I came out of the Silence unable to take a deep enough breath to satisfy my empty lungs. I lay on the dirt path, staring up at the tops of the trees while I struggled to recover. My head was pounding. I gradually sat up and assessed how far I'd come. The line I'd drawn was barely visible. I'd made it forty or fifty feet, which hardly seemed worth it for the instant killer hangover. I was definitely not ready to try that again for a while.

It was oddly disappointing to learn there was a limit to my new ability. It felt like only limitless power could protect me the next time Britt found my hiding place.

I'll keep at it. I have to get stronger.

Being stronger. Being free. They felt like goals, but they also felt like memories. I wanted to live those memories again.

Maybe I had the beginning of a plan after all.

Looking up, the top of the mountain suddenly seemed farther away than when I started my experiments. I decided to make the hike up another day when I wasn't pushing my limits in the Silence. I turned back for the cabin earlier than I'd planned but satisfied with what I'd accomplished. It felt good to reach a milestone again, even if it was a small one. I was always happier trying to figure out how things worked.

BACK INSIDE THE cabin after my walk, I grabbed my phone from the bedroom dresser to catch up on the day's news. I ended up seeing my apartment finder app first. It had felt like the first small victory when I installed it back in La Grange, the first time it felt like I was really leaving. Now, here I was again facing a choice of where to go. I clicked on the icon, not really sure whether I was truly interested in taking that first step again or not. My finger hovered over the search button.

The phone vibrated as the screen announced an incoming call. I jumped. Thankfully, it was just Gemma's number calling and not Britt using her one phone call. I pressed the button to answer.

"Hey there," I said.

A shuffling noise answered on the other end. I wondered

if she'd maybe called me by accident. Then, a weak voice drifted over the line. "Zoe? You're there?"

"I'm here." My body went on alert. I didn't like the disassociation in her voice. "Is everything all right?"

More shuffling on her end before a distant pounding sounded, like someone banging on a door. Gemma fell silent until it stopped.

"What's going on?" I asked. "Are you okay?"

"No," she answered. A painfully long silence followed. I wanted to throw the phone down to find her and help. If worse came to worst, I could use the old pickup Gemma's family kept in the shed outside.

"What's happening?" I asked.

She laughed, only for a breath. "I thought I could hold out. I can't. It's time."

"Time for what? Gemma, I don't understand what this is about."

"Amaryn," she said.

As soon as I heard her name, my heart sank. I feared the worst. "Did something happen to her?"

Gemma laughed again, the only audience to her joke. It was a tired laugh. A detached laugh.

"The hospital went back on their word," she said. "Their *word*. Said it has gone on too long. They want me to let her die. I won't let them. Won't let them murder her. Can't."

While Gemma talked, I began to search frantically for the keys to the old truck. I tried to keep her talking while I looked.

"We're going to get her through this," I said. I immediately hated myself for the lie.

"Just promise," Gemma replied. She paused again. Another round of knocking sounded from the background. "Promise me you'll keep Amaryn out of the hands of the people who'll try to take her. The World Union. Valhalla."

"Gemma?" *Oh gods, she's going to do something to get herself killed.*

"Zoe, I'm going to give her a dose of Chaos."

This time it was my turn to go silent. Chaos wasn't something you just bottled and used like medicine. It was predatory. "No. No. Gemma, you can't do this. You don't know what it'll do."

"This is the only option," Gemma replied. "Remember, Zoe. If I'm not there to protect her, you need to be."

The line went dead.

"Damn it!"

I frantically tried to get her back on the line. Her voicemail picked up before the first ring. She wasn't in her right mind, and she was about to do something that had a better chance to turn Amaryn into another Cedric than help her. If I got there quickly, I could convince Gemma to look for another hospital that might take her, or I could at least convince her to let me take a blood sample for study before she went through with an injection of Chaos—anything to stop what was about to happen.

I rushed from room to room until I found the keys to the truck and then hurried to the barn. The truck had half a tank of gas—hopefully enough to make it back to Seattle. Rusted hinges screamed for mercy as I opened the door to climb inside.

Once I got on the highway, I drove as fast as the old engine would take me. Seattle came into view just as I cleared Snoqualmie Pass. I took the Front Street exit and followed the signs until I got to the hospital. I nearly ran through the lobby, making my best effort not to look like the frenzied woman I was. My fingers fumbled over the elevator buttons. The ride to the fourth floor felt like I'd inadvertently flexed and paused time.

The doors opened. I ran down the hall to room 417, bypassing the nurse's station where a pair of nurses yelled after me to stop and sign in. I banged my hand on the door. "Gemma? Gemma, it's me, Zoe."

To my surprise, the door moved. Without speaking, Gemma pulled the door open and stepped back to let me through. As soon as I was in the room, she let the door drift close again, refusing to make eye contact with me. She backed up until her legs brushed against the couch before folding herself onto the cushions. Her eyes were puffed, bloodshot, and ringed in dark shadows.

The entry to Amaryn's room stood halfway open. The steady hum of machines drifted from inside. I walked past Gemma to check her daughter's room.

I'm too late.

The bedcovers had been pulled back from Amaryn's right arm, which hung limp in between the bedrails. Her IV machine had been pulled beside her shoulder. There, lying empty on the floor, was a glass lab sample container with a rubber stopper at the end. A spent syringe had been cast beside it.

"It didn't work," Gemma said in a weak voice from the other room.

A machine chimed the passing of another mechanical breath forced through her daughter's lungs.

"It was supposed to *work.*" Gemma let her face fall into her hands. She shuddered, tears flowing along the sides of her fingers.

CHAPTER TEN

GEMMA EVENTUALLY FELL asleep on the couch around midnight. There was no small amount of irony in feeling powerless as I stood there in the center of the hospital suite, trying to figure out how I could help. When I put myself in her shoes, I immediately felt the crushing wave of reality she must be enduring. What Gemma and Amaryn needed was something I couldn't give them—time.

Another dose of irony. I headed into the treatment room, sensing the inevitable conclusion to Amaryn's sad fate.

The emptied vial of Chaos still lay on the floor beside Amaryn's bed. Without Gemma in the room, being there was like walking through someone else's house when they weren't at home. It was cold and quiet except for the steady rhythm of the ventilator. Amaryn's emaciated arm hung through the sides of the bed railing. Her sheets were pulled back across her chest, giving me an unwanted view of what the disease had done to her. The hospital gown nearly swallowed her whole. The best I could do to stay focused was to try to keep my eyes off her while I covered up her mom's mistake.

A pile of used alcohol wipes and gauzes beside Amaryn's bed marked the scene of Gemma's lapse of reason. I knelt to collect it all. The last thing Gemma needed was the hospital staff asking questions. If anyone found out what she'd done, she'd be banned from ever working in research again—if she managed to stay out of prison.

Holding the empty vial felt like holding a spent bullet casing. I stole a quick look at Amaryn's arm hanging beside me. The crook of her elbow was perfectly uniform in its pale complexion. There was no trace of the shot, just as there was no trace on me when it absorbed through my skin. I took a deep breath and moved her arm back under the sheets as fast as I could. It was worse than handling a cadaver. Her muscles were flaccid and atrophied, her skin loose and cold. I hit the metal of the guardrail when I jerked my hand away. I'd seen plenty of dead bodies during my time in bio-med labs, but I'd never been in the same room as someone on the precipice of becoming a corpse. This was someone I didn't know and yet I wanted to pull her back, away from the rapidly approaching edge. I could only imagine how overwhelming the same urge must have been for Gemma—more so when she couldn't do anything but watch Amaryn slide further away.

I stowed the empty vial in my pocket and put the machines back where I thought they'd been before. The room looked somewhat back to normal, enough so that the hospital staff wouldn't add to Gemma's woes with a lawsuit before they took away Amaryn's life support. It felt so unfair and inhumane to decide to remove someone's tether to hope just to satisfy some arbitrary rules.

Gemma stirred on the couch. Even sleeping, she looked haggard and overwhelmed with grief. *There's got to be more I can do to help her*. I looked down at my hands, flexing fingers that could touch something and freeze it in time, and yet were useless against a system of rules that dictated whether people lived or died.

Maybe those rules were the key, though. Rules were made by people, and these people didn't have all the information they needed to decide Amaryn's fate. If I could talk to someone making those choices and show them there was a potential for a cure, I could convince them to give Gemma and Amaryn more time. Just a few more days would help. Anything to keep Gemma from making another choice that might get her arrested, while at the same time giving me a window to uncover a key to Chaos. It was worth a shot.

I made my way out of the room quietly to find one of the doctors. The nurses' station gave off a warm yellow glow midway between two open waiting areas. The chairs and couches sat empty. It still seemed strange that no one else appeared to be occupying the ward besides Amaryn. I hadn't heard so much as a cough out of any of the adjoining rooms.

"Can I help you?" A middle-aged brunette with tight curls stretched into a ponytail peaked her head over the station wall.

"Actually, yes. I—" I leaned on the counter next to her console only to realize mid-sentence that she was wearing a Valhalla Security uniform.

She rested her hands on her hips, just above a neural gun holster. "You must be Zoe."

Shit.

I immediately flexed into the Silence. The glow from my skin reflected in her eyes. Her mouth showed the beginning of a smile—a smile I imagined would widen after she took aim at me. I didn't have time to figure out why Valhalla was at the hospital. I was within reach of her gun if I stretched my arm, so I switched it off as soon as my fingers grazed the handle. I stepped back and got as far from the counter as I could before I had to let loose of my flex. It was enough of a head start.

"Hey!" I could hear the guard struggling to get free after I turned to run.

Just past Amaryn's suite, another guard walked through the elevator doors at the end of the hall with a rifle slung across his back.

I stopped so fast I nearly fell. The man glared at me like he wasn't sure what he was looking at, and then the recognition hit.

Cornered.

I turned back toward the nurse's station and let out a surprised scream as I ran face-first into Gemma.

"What's going on?" she asked. Mascara smudges darkened the skin beneath her eyes.

Gemma surveyed the guards. The one by the nurse's station had taken off her holster to stand in front of the desk. The other looked like he was waiting for Gemma to move so he could get a clear shot. Gemma didn't bat an eye. She put her hand on my back and guided me toward the door. "Come back inside."

She led me into the suite. I took one final look at the guards, sure that they would follow.

"You can relax," she said, letting the door glide shut. "They're not here for you."

"How do you know that?"

"Because I sent for them."

My first thought was that she'd turned on me, leading the wolves right to my door because I was of no use to her now, but that couldn't have been true. I never would have made it out of the elevator if she didn't want me to be there.

"I made a deal with the board," she said, heading off my questions. "You're safe with me."

And only with me. She didn't say it, but it was implied. "What are they doing here?" I asked. I cast another glance at the door to make sure they really weren't coming inside.

"They're security officers. They're keeping the floor secure."

"The hospital has people that do that."

"My point, exactly. I needed to be sure no one from the hospital could interfere."

I chose my next words carefully. By the undercurrents of tension in her voice, I was walking through an increasingly crowded minefield. "I can't pretend to know how hard this is for you, but this is a public hospital. You can't just keep them out."

"I can and I will," she snapped back. "Those worthless bastards. I paid an obscene amount of money to rent this floor. The hospital agreed—in no uncertain terms—that Amaryn's care was not to be stopped. They reneged on that deal. I did what I had to do."

"You rented an entire floor?"

She ran a hand through her matted hair. I could almost feel it tugging against her knots. "The company did, technically. I needed a capable team to care for Amaryn, and Valhalla had the means. They won't miss a few pennies."

That explained why the floor was so empty. I put my hand on my hips. She was digging a hole for herself that I wasn't sure she could get out of. "Gemma, this is… Maybe this has gone too far."

"Excuse me?" The words came out in a constrained shudder.

"I'm sorry, but—"

"I don't want to hear how sorry you are. How about a *thank you*, Zoe? I would think a little gratitude would be in order after all I've done for you."

My instinct was to grovel immediately, to fall down at Gemma's feet and beg her to not take out her anger on me. Going against what Britt had instilled felt like trying to stop an avalanche with a baby gate, but I did the best I could to keep some semblance of self-worth. "It's just a lot to take in. What you're doing with Amaryn—spending Valhalla's money for all this, stealing the Chaos—you could get in a lot of trouble."

She looked at me like she didn't understand the concept. "Who's going to say anything? We've got a blank check to decode Chaos. Considering what I've lived through lately, I don't think you'd begrudge me calling this a research expense."

"I don't think that's how others will see it, especially the board."

"The board will see what I *tell* them to see."

Her words had a finality to them, delivered with such an abrupt tone that it was clear she considered the matter closed. "Honestly, Zoe, I can't believe this is what's troubling you. I'm sitting here not ten feet away from my dying daughter and the monsters at this hospital tell me I have twenty-four hours to find another place for her. None of the hospitals I called will take her. What would you have done?"

She reached inside her purse to take out a medicine bottle, removing the lid in a single motion with the ease of someone who's been opening bottles her whole life. She downed the pills dry.

While I couldn't imagine the pressures she was under, she was in no state to be making rational decisions. I didn't even want to think about what she'd do if the hospital tried to force their way onto the floor.

The only way I could keep the situation from exploding was to show that I could potentially control Chaos. Maybe that would give the hospital—and Gemma—the proof they needed to stand down. Doing it in less than a day sounded next to impossible. I had to try though.

I looked back at the door and considered the guards on the other side who were supposedly not a threat to me anymore. I needed more than a few borrowed microscopes at the lake house if I wanted to make a difference. And since Valhalla was temporarily off my back, I had an idea how.

"There might be something I could do," I said.

"It's too late for you to help me now."

"There's still time. Let me see the files on Cedric and the others," I replied.

Gemma froze. I'd never seen her look anything close to scared before, but her eyes widened like I'd turned into a ghost. "No," she said. "Absolutely not."

"But they could help."

"I said *no*, Zoe." She seemed to catch herself after the words came out under a thick layer of venom. She even tried to smile. "It's just that they're sealed, that's all. Some of the families are trying to sue us. Part of their grief, sure, but it means we're not allowed access to them anymore."

"Are the files still at Valhalla?"

"Yes, but I can't get to them. No one can. The WU has them under constant surveillance. It's not possible."

Not possible. Those were words I questioned now. I had an idea, but I couldn't bring myself to tell her everything. It was better to keep from adding more worries to her pile. "Then give me some time tonight to study her cancer. Let me build a case for the hospital to reconsider. If there's some way my power can help—or at least extend her time—I want to try."

Gemma looked toward the door to Amaryn's room. It was the first time in recent memory where I couldn't detect a hint of optimism in her eyes. She was in the process of saying goodbye.

"I'll call you tomorrow morning when I know something," I said. "I'll be at the house."

She nodded, then laid back down on the couch without answering. It was my cue to leave, but I wasn't going back to the lake house.

I was headed to Valhalla.

CHAPTER ELEVEN

GET IN, *find the files, get out.*

Sitting in the 24-hour coffee shop across the street from Valhalla Tower, I tried to psych myself up for heading back inside. Looking up at the sixty floors of black mirrored exterior, all I could see was a prison now. It was hard to believe that at one time I'd expected to find so much hope in it.

Now here I was, trying to find it again.

My coffee tasted just like I expected a 3am cup would—bitter and way too hot—but it was mostly there for me to hold while I went over the various ways my plan could go wrong. It didn't matter that Gemma had negotiated a deal to keep the guards off my back. I wasn't ready to trust them to keep their word. To them, I was lost property. And I still hadn't forgotten the looks on the guards' faces when I made my escape—wild fear mixed with resentment for having dared to slip their grasp. They'd had no hesitation about using weapons against me. Back then, they treated me like a threat. Now I would be.

The more I thought about my plan, the more I started to admit that some part of me was doing it to find out what happened to the rest of the people like me—Cedric and the others who were infected before I arrived. As much as I wanted to figure out the key to Chaos, I also wanted to know what fate I'd avoided.

Get in, find the files, get out, I repeated to myself. The finale of my pep talk was a sip of bitter coffee that was almost bad enough to chase off the fog of procrastination. I let my eyes linger on the front door of the monolithic skyscraper. *Am I really going to do this?* I pictured Amaryn slowly wasting away at home after being denied the medical help she needed. I pictured what that would do to Gemma, who was already showing signs of cracking under the stress. There was no telling what she would do in the death throes of hope. Of course I was going to do this.

I got up and tossed the empty cup into the recycling on my way out the door. Outside, I craned my neck to look up to the lights still shining in Valhalla's fortieth-floor suite.

Looks like somebody's home. Yay.

I took out the tie holding my ponytail and shook out my hair until it was a tumbleweed framing both sides of my face. It was the best I could do for camouflage on short notice. The fewer people who recognized me, the better. Despite the obviously foolproof disguise, I was ready to slip into the Silence at the first sign of trouble. Paranoia, no matter how justified, was not a good recipe for looking casual. I forced a yawn as I walked through the door to get out some of the nerves while trying to fit into the crowd and ended up sounding like a rusty car door in the relative quiet of the lobby. I might as well have played entrance music. I hurried toward the elevators like a rat who stumbled into the light.

"Good morning, Zoe," a man at the front desk said with a plastered grin.

My body crackled with nervous energy. I stopped mid-stride, expecting a horde of security guards to rush in at any moment.

The man's smile never wavered. "Wonderful to see you

again." Beyond his forced grin was a subtle shift to his eyes, as though he were speaking to a live bomb that might go off at the slightest annoyance.

"I didn't know I was expected."

Another uncomfortable shift whisked away by a superficial laugh. "Just…happy to see you."

The man at the desk fidgeted like he was in the middle of the line of fire and couldn't wait for me to move so a sniper could shoot. Everything inside told me to run, but there was something else in the man's expression, something mixed with the fear. It was like a bank teller who was being robbed. He just wanted me to take the money and go, which is exactly what I meant to do.

I searched the people standing around the lobby, looking for the faces of the men who'd chased me the first time, especially the one who fired the neural gun on me in the stairwell. There wasn't a single guard, not even a stray night watchman wandering the crowd.

A couple in suits cut their glances away from me as we made eye contact. They made a quick diversion toward the exit.

"Ms. Weeks told us to make sure you have whatever lab equipment you need," the guard said.

My muscles tensed. Gemma had known I would come. The part of me left jaded by years of veiled threats took that to mean she knew exactly why I was there, but I wasn't ready to believe it. Maybe she was trying to protect me, in her own way.

"Anything you need help carrying, you let me know and I'll make sure it happens." He paused. "Is that okay?"

The man looked like he was on the edge of panic, as if one wrong word might make me explode. The phone next to his keyboard rang. He reached for it greedily on the first ring.

I held the receiver down. "Just one question. Since when do you take orders from Gemma Weeks?"

His eyes narrowed before he let out a nervous scoff. The phone chimed again. "Do you mind?"

I pulled my hand away. He answered his call, leaving me lead-footed in place.

Looking toward the elevators, I felt like an animal staring into the mouth of a trap. If I was going to run, that was my moment, but what kept me in place was the thought of what would happen if I did run again. I'd seen what Gemma's desperation had led to. She'd already played with fire once. If I didn't do something to stop that now, the fire she started could burn everything to the ground. It would follow me no matter where I tried to run to.

My senses were on high alert. The emptiness of the lobby meant every step someone took sounded like cymbals crashing next to my ears. The few people there were gave me an extra wide berth as I walked toward the elevators. A few of them tried to put on a welcoming smile, but they were no better at hiding their fear than the guy at the desk.

The palm scanner for the fortieth floor elevator sat in front of me. I placed my hand on the screen, honestly not sure if it would still work. The red light drifted over my palm. A few seconds later, the elevator doors parted. I stepped inside and pressed the button to take me up to the labs.

When the doors opened, the front desk clerk sat alone behind her desk in the lobby. She looked at me with a fragile smile. "Welcome back," she said.

I took a slow look around for an ambush before stepping out of the elevator. As soon as I did, the woman picked up her phone and pressed a button.

I was too far away to stop her from sounding the alarm. Instead, I kept close to the elevator to see what she'd do.

She held the bottom of the phone just below her mouth. "She's here." She placed the receiver back gently, never taking her eyes off me.

The elevator doors drifted shut. I waited for the rush of

guards, ready to enter the Silence at the first sign of a neural gun, but instead, Anjo—the Staff Manager from my first day—got up from his desk across the office floor and navigated the sea of half-wall cubicles to meet me at the front. His hand had a tremor as he waved hello. He had a thin bead of sweat just below his receding hairline.

These people think I'm going to kill them.

"I can take you back," he said. He pointed over his shoulder to the labs.

"After you."

I followed him through the labyrinth of cubes, my head on a swivel as I kept watch for the guards. The further I got from the elevator, the more I realized I was coming to the hardest part of my plan. I couldn't get a bead on how Gemma knowing I was there would change things. I assumed she was the one to get Anjo out of bed to babysit me. Now I needed to find a way to ditch my tour guide.

There were more people than I expected working third shift. To a person, they sat at their desks desperately trying not to let themselves be seen gawking. If I did manage to make eye contact, they pretended to be too busy to notice.

"Awfully crowded in here for ass o'clock on a Tuesday," I said.

Anjo looked back with a half grin that lasted only until he turned away again. He stopped at the lab door and put his fingers on the handle. "Here we are."

"Wait," I said. I didn't like that I couldn't see what waited on the other side.

He froze without looking back.

"Is there someone waiting for me back there?"

He turned the handle and pulled the door open. "Nobody's that stupid."

I started to wonder what kind of stories had circulated about me since the last time I was here. Everyone seemed so afraid.

I glanced through the doorway, seeing the long hall that led back to Gemma's office. My lab and the rest of the research facilities were to the left. I couldn't get over the sense of being watched, and not just by the cameras that would maneuver to track me once I got into the halls. I could feel the stares behind me, the wary eyes of people watching an escaped animal roam freely through their space.

Just in case Gemma's assigned guide wasn't totally being honest, I entered the Silence and took a few strained steps into the hallway to make sure nothing was there. It all seemed empty.

Anjo's surprised expression held the reflection of my light in his eyes. I relaxed my flex and came back to hear him finish the gasp.

"I can take it from here," I said.

"I'm supposed to…help," he replied. Sweat started to darken the edges of his hair. The poor guy flinched at my every move.

"It's okay, you know. I'm not going to hurt you."

He couldn't look me in the eye for more than an instant.

"I know my way to the lab," I said.

He shifted on his feet. "Ms. Weeks said you'd need help carrying stuff, since you're getting lab equipment."

"I will. But first I want to check on some things." I started down the hallway toward the part of the research wing I hadn't been to before.

"The lab's not…" He drifted off, looking like he couldn't decide who was the more dangerous person to piss off—Gemma or me.

"I thought you managed company staff," I said, stopping.

"I do."

"Then what's got you so worried?"

He blinked quickly and looked around like the answer eluded him. "There's nothing for you down there. All records are digital, even the backups. It's off limits."

So, Gemma did know why I was there. The nervousness I felt at being found out was quickly replaced by frustration and curiosity. It was starting to seem like there was more to it than a few legal issues that were making her so scared. People who guarded information that closely always rubbed me the wrong way.

"Is it off limits for you?" I asked, pointing down the hall.

Anjo's hand fell to his waist, where he seemed to unconsciously hide the ID card attached to a badge reel. A black band ran across the bottom corner of the card. When his hand touched it, the band lit up with four digital numbers. It looked exactly like the kind of entry key I would need to get where I was going.

"Is that the key card?" I asked.

"No," he said.

"Then what is it?"

"Nothing."

"If it was nothing you wouldn't lie about it."

"Please," he said. "Just do what you need to do in the labs and leave. There's nothing in Containment. I don't want this."

"Containment?"

He caught his breath and slowly shut his eyes. The poor guy looked like he was about to cry.

"Look, I'm just trying to help Ms. Weeks," I said, attempting to calm him. "If there's something back there I can use to study Chaos, I need to see it."

He shook his head. "I can't let you. And whatever you're looking for, it's not worth it."

"It'll be okay, trust me."

"No, it won't." He said the words so surely, as if he was looking down into the grave I was about to dig for myself.

"What are you talking about?"

"How do you think she got where she is?" He looked around the hall like the question might set off an alarm. His voice sank. "Her husband used to run this place, you know. *Used to.*"

The news wasn't as much of a shock to my system as he might've thought. It was no wonder she had as much influence as she did at Valhalla. Now it made sense how she'd been able to make the deal to keep security off my back. *But if she had that power, why had they tried to stop me in the first place?* I didn't like where that road led. I didn't want to believe that about Gemma.

But should I?

"I know about her husband," I said finally. "She told me."

"She told you the whole story? Then you know how he died. You know what she does to people who *disappoint.*"

A response never made it to my lips. *Dead?* She never said anything about that. Anjo had been guarding each word like she was standing behind him listening this whole time, and it finally dawned on me that the man wasn't afraid of my power. None of them were. They were afraid of Gemma's.

I didn't like the unsteady ground I suddenly found myself on. I didn't know who to trust anymore, but I would sort out the lies later. Neither the hospital staff nor Amaryn were to blame for Gemma's secrets, and they needed my help.

"Sorry about this," I said.

"About what?"

I entered the Silence and took his key card out of the flow of time. I made sure I wasn't in the same place when I came back.

As soon as I relaxed my hold, Anjo searched and found me a few feet from where he'd just seen me and panicked like I hoped he would. He stumbled backward, his fall snapping the card from his belt. It remained stationary in mid-air.

I re-entered the Silence and switched it back on again. The card fell into my hand.

"Thanks."

"Wait!" he called after as I started down the hall, but there was no turning back now. I needed to see whatever secrets Gemma was trying so hard to keep from me.

I FIGURED I had at least a couple of minutes before Anjo told his tale to Gemma, and she had Security come after me again. I hurried down the winding hall of the Containment wing, checking each door, but none of them had a keypad where I could enter the numbers coming up on Anjo's card.

The farther I got, the more unsettlingly familiar my surroundings became. I rounded the final corner, and it was like I'd stepped back in time after escaping the containment room. I recognized the hallway where I'd come out of my cell. The door to the office where I made my escape loomed on the right. It was like walking through a scar, each step pulling at the barely healed wound.

I didn't have time to dwell on the memory. I kept checking doors, searching for any sort of screen that would accept a password. Finally, I came to one set apart from the rest—a heavy steel door with a single keypad above the handle. The hallway was still quiet, but I knew it wouldn't stay that way for long. I touched the black screen to bring the password prompt to life. A flashing red cursor waited for my entry. I typed in the numbers currently on Anjo's card. A sound like hydraulics releasing pressure came from inside the lock mechanism, ending in a clank as the locks receded. I couldn't help a smile. The universe had come through for once. I pulled the handle and slipped inside.

A dull red overhead light painted the narrow room with an unsettling crimson veneer. Three nondescript doors ran alongside one wall. There were no windows to see inside. Beside each door hung a plastic tray, each labeled with single numbers—one, two, and three. The two closest to me had black notebooks sitting in them. I found the third notebook lying on a table at the end of the room next to a small video monitor, silent and dusty.

None of the doors had handles. I knocked gently on the middle door. Something moved on the other side.

This wasn't a closet for file storage, it was a prison, and there might be people like me inside the cells.

I had an urge to set them loose, no longer an animal to be kept in a cage like I was. A sobering thought kept my hands at my side—what if they were too dangerous to release? I closed my eyes. At some point, another person standing outside a door like this had asked the same question about me.

Get a move on, Zoe. I forced myself to get back to the job at hand. I slipped one of the binders out of the tray, but before I could open it, footsteps pounded from outside the door. I looked outside and recognized the guard's face immediately. It was the same man who'd tried to shoot me during my escape. Anjo was close on his heels.

I'd come too far to let them stop me now. I pushed the door shut and then flexed to freeze it in place. I could deal with them when I was done.

The dull sound of fists beating against the immovable door faded to background noise as I opened the binder. Each page looked like a novel written in an alien language. There were no letters, only strange hicroglyphics and brokcn symbols, almost as if someone tried to print out the pages with only a few drops of ink in the printer. Nothing made sense, no matter how many sections I flipped through. I tried the next binder. More symbols. Defeated, I took a look at the last folder on the table, the one that happened to have the most pages. I had no doubt that what I was looking at held information on Chaos; I just needed to figure out how to decipher it.

I flipped through some of the pages, which were as frustratingly unhelpful as the rest. Without the key to decipher the data, it was worthless. I took out my phone and snapped a few pictures anyway to run through an image search later.

Another fist hitting steel rang in my ear, but it wasn't from the guard outside. Whoever was behind the door next to me rapped their fist against the metal.

"Who's there?" I asked.

They slammed their fist against the door hard enough to rattle the light overhead. If these were the people who were infected before me, they clearly weren't dead or in comas like Gemma said. And they were clearly powerful. Judging by how much she'd apparently been lying to me, there was no judge, no World Union lawyer keeping the records sealed.

I took the binder off the desk and gripped it tight. I didn't care how much power she wielded at Valhalla; I was headed back to the hospital to get whatever cipher I needed to read the files. If she wouldn't give it to me, I would take what I found to the World Union and let her deal with the fallout. I was done being lied to.

The guard outside stopped knocking. There would be more like him coming soon. It was time for me to go.

Before I left, I paused at the middle door. It felt wrong to leave them here, dangerous or not. *I'll come back for you*, I silently promised as I laid my hand on the cell.

My focus shifted to the frozen door. Whoever was on the other side would be prepared for me, so I had to be prepared for them. I held the binder over my chest to use as a temporary shield in case they brought neural guns again. Even a grazing shot could knock me out cold for hours, and now I'd seen what waited for me if they got a hold of me again. After taking a breath, I flexed and switched time back on for the door. I came back to the room prepared for them to barge in, but the door stayed closed. Outside, the hallway sounded calm.

I pulled quickly on the handle and held the binder tight, ready to flex. The guard stood facing me carrying something that looked like a cross between a flame thrower and a fire extinguisher, with a barrel that ended in a wide nozzle attached to a hefty canister. I entered the Silence as soon as I saw him start to take aim.

Somewhere in the time between starting my flex and riding past the wave of nausea, an explosion of smoke from the end of the giant gun filled the doorway. A thick stream of chalky gray liquid pierced the cloud's center. I panicked at first because the immovability of things in the Silence meant the smoke from the blast could block my way past the guard, but I found enough room near the bottom to escape. Before I ducked through, though, I wanted to freeze whatever it was that was coming out of the gun. It looked like it was still connected to the barrel, which was just beyond my reach. I could think of a dozen things that chalky stuff might do if it hit me and none of them were good. Putting my finger to the white surface, I barely felt the spark of time within the object. I tried again and felt the same weak signal, like I was only touching a flake of snow in an avalanche. I leaned in for a closer look. What I'd thought was a solid wave of liquid was actually thousands of tiny pellets. Freezing a single pellet in the stream would do nothing.

Shit.

Studying the cloud had taken too long. My hold on the Silence was slipping. I ducked beneath the droplets and moved to the edge of my bubble of time, just to the right of the guard's legs. It felt like thousands of tiny hooks scratching at my muscles every inch I stretched toward my limit. I let go just as I edged past the man and came back to an explosion of noise. A wave of pellets engulfed the room as they expanded into a rigid foam that filled the space. The binder that had been in my hand stood pinned against the back wall as the foam crept over it. I didn't even realize it hadn't come into the Silence with me. Now I'd lost the one thing I came for.

"You didn't kill her, right?" Anjo said from the opposite side of the guard. "She said to keep her alive if we can."

If we can? I should've been running, but the realization of what he'd said kept me in place. How could she? I was here to help her daughter.

"Beside you!"

Anjo jabbed a pointing finger at me. I had to move. The hulking guard checked over his shoulder and then rounded on me with the pellet launcher swinging toward my face.

I scrambled to get back to my feet—hyper aware of how much time I was wasting just fumbling to stand—and took off toward the exit, rounding turns with the drumming of footsteps following. The snaking hallway was the only thing keeping me from getting blanketed by the foam. I made it back to the hallway that ended in the door to the office—a long, straight dash with no turns to protect me. I didn't pay much attention when we were here before, but once I saw how far down the door was, I started to realize that there was no way I could outrun whatever they shot at me. It was too far.

I could time walk. It seemed like it might work, but what I'd done back in the woods wouldn't get me halfway from where I was, so I stretched my legs with each stride, pushing myself to get as far as I could before he got another shot off. Then the trailing footsteps stopped. I could sense the attack coming. I was so close to a distance I could cover but it still seemed far away. The guard took away my choice. As soon as I heard the cannon shot go off, I re-entered the Silence.

The slices of time mocked me with a view of the doorway not thirty feet away, stretching toward infinity. I looked behind me, hoping the cloud of pellets hadn't made their way to me yet, and nearly let go of my flex after seeing how close they were. The burst of pellets was already halfway down the hall. Even if they missed me, they'd hit the door and block my only way out. My only hope was to move while nothing else could —I had to time walk.

Facing the end of the hallway again, I pushed myself four, five, then a painful six steps beyond where I entered. I braced myself against the nausea and crippling pain as I moved to the maximum distance from my entry point. It was time to let go. As soon as the pressure became too much, I relaxed—and then immediately flexed again.

The cannon shot had only moved by a few feet, giving me a chance to make it closer to the door. Just like it had in the woods, the pain from my previous trip into the Silence disappeared as soon as I made my re-entry, but it only took a few steps for it to reappear. My hold on the Silence started to slip faster with each re-entry. I couldn't let that worry take over. I had to keep going.

Relax. Flex. Move.

Relax. Flex. Move.

I would hear flashes of the gunshot's echo as I moved through the stop-motion diorama. It was like being in a room where someone kept hitting mute on the TV volume. I imagined what I must look like to the two men who saw me appear and disappear like one of those flip books I played with as a kid. Despite my progress, the cannon shot was only an arm's length behind me now. The accumulated pain of my trips tore at the unseen tendons connecting me to the Silence. The door stood only a step away. Its frame filled the slices of my vision.

I only had one more time step to go before I was to the door. When I left the Silence and went back in, I could feel the first brushes of the pellets touching the back of my neck. I pushed myself to get within reach of the handle. As soon as my fingers could take hold, I let go of the Silence for good. In the rush of sound and nausea, I turned the handle and fell through the door's opening. The pellets hit the door and immediately bloomed into a wall of chalky white. The hallway was blocked, trapping Anjo and his bodyguard on the other side.

I lost each breath as fast as I could inhale, my body debilitated from the stuttered trip across the hallway. But I was safe—for the moment.

One aching joint at a time, I managed to stand on two feet again. The handful of people milling about the office took turns stealing looks at me. I didn't have the energy to pretend I was anything other than exhausted. My chest ached. My legs could barely keep me upright. I felt like if I laid back down on the floor, I could sleep for days.

"Slight mishap in the lab," I said, thumbing over my shoulder. "I'll get a mop."

Through the sea of stunned, silent looks, I hobbled my way to the elevator, each step a painful memory of stretching the boundaries of the Silence. The thought of entering it again made my already-tired muscles tense in pain. If the guards came through another door to take me down, there wasn't much I could do. I didn't have the strength to hold on to a flex.

The woman from the front desk stood in the open elevator ahead of me, a bag slung over her shoulder. If Gemma made her get up at the crack of dawn to greet me, this woman clearly felt her task was over. I limped through the sliding doors and collapsed with my back against the wall. With each breath, I slowly emerged from exhaustion.

As the doors slid shut, she glanced over her shoulder. She cleared her throat and switched her bag from one shoulder to the other.

"Thanks for waiting," I said, still panting.

"Sure," she replied, and turned to face the door again after giving me a long glance. She reached down and slowly lifted the phone from her pocket.

I didn't have time or energy for dealing with Gemma's spy network. I flexed and froze her phone in place. The resurgent pain and nausea were worth it for the high-pitched shriek she let out as soon as I came back.

"I'll save you the call," I said as the doors slid open. "I'm on my way to see her now."

WHILE THE RECEPTIONIST stood horrified at the sight of her phone frozen in air, I eyed the man at the desk on my way out, trying my best to make him scared of me instead of his boss.

He didn't make a move to stop me.

I was so mad thinking about the depths of Gemma's lies, my pounding steps could've left footprints in the concrete. I should've run the second Britt found me, but it wasn't too late to fix that mistake. If I'd only trusted my instincts about Gemma, I could've been in another city-state by now. But I couldn't leave yet. There was something in those files about Chaos that Gemma was hiding, something that might be able to help me control it. *Or cure it.* And then there was Amaryn. She was the only innocent party in all this. No doubt Gemma would have her bodyguards waiting for me when I got there, but I was too pissed to let anyone get in my way. I would get my answers about Cedric and the others and use them to help Amaryn if I could—Gemma be damned—but then I would move on. I couldn't be in another relationship, even a professional one, where I was constantly fed half-truths and manipulations.

My stamina had almost fully recovered by the time I got to the hospital. I entered the building and rode the elevator up to the third floor, ready to do another time walk to get past the guards if I had to. Then it would be me, Gemma, and a frozen door lock until I got what I came for.

The doors opened. As soon as I got a view of the hallway, I saw the Valhalla guard who had been at the nurse's desk earlier. She was running toward me. I flexed as soon as I realized who she was. Her image split into infinite versions of herself, mid-stride to take me down. I stepped beyond the elevator door and moved slightly to one side. When I came back out of the Silence, she ran straight past me through the doors. I readied myself to flex again, but she didn't seem to care that she missed. The woman repeatedly jammed the floor buttons. When the doors started to close, she looked nervously back out into hall. She only paid attention to me when the doors were nearly shut.

"Run," she muttered.

The elevator closed.

I turned and stared down the hallway toward Amaryn's room. My eyes fixated on the room door, left halfway open. Faint silhouettes moved across the carpet outside. They were hypnotic, holding my stare as I walked quietly toward the opening. The dead air of the empty hallway stoked the sense of wrongness. I got to the door and curled myself around the opening. The couch was empty. The TV on the wall flickered as ribbons of static silently rained down the display. The room was filled with white noise.

I switched the TV off. A twinkling sound took its place, like a child's toy slowly running out of battery.

The lock to Amaryn's recovery room clicked. The door started to open, creeping wider until I could see that no one was on the other side pushing it. I stepped closer, my mind racing as I tried to imagine what waited in the darkness.

Slowly, Gemma came into view, sitting at the end of the empty hospital bed. Amaryn sat in a wooden rocker by the window, a familiar shade of red glowing beneath wilted eyelids. Dark patches like bruises covered the top of her exposed shoulders. Gemma reached out and stroked her matted hair, alternating between sobs and choked laughter as the knots caught in her fingers. She twisted her head toward me. There was a pause before I saw recognition in her eyes.

"It worked," she said, fresh tears dislodged by her jerky laugh. "Zoe, it *worked*."

Her eyes cut from me to the table at the back of the room. A wooden music box sat on top. Inside, a porcelain ballerina twisted in time to the wailing chorus of metallic notes. In between the melody, a child's voice drifted from the belly of the toy.

"*Mommy… Mommy, it's me. I love you.*

Mommy… Mommy, it's me. I love you."

"My baby," Gemma said, her manic voice chained in whispers. "My Amaryn."

CHAPTER TWELVE

Behind me, the child's voice droned from the music box. *Mommy, it's me. I love you.*

"What you couldn't." Gemma smiled triumphantly as she studied Amaryn's face. The steady glow of Chaos still burned beneath the girl's eyelids. "I saved her. Didn't I, love?"

I placed a hand over the music box, bringing the dancing figure's song to a stop. The room fell quiet. Gemma barely noticed at first, only to turn and glare at me with an indignant scowl.

"You need to tell me what happened here," I said. "Whatever Chaos did to her, we don't understand it. She could be dangerous."

"Worried you're not special anymore?" Gemma squeezed Amaryn's hand. "I couldn't let the hospital renege on their promise, and you were taking too long to do what I hired you to do. Maybe if you weren't so careless, you could've done more. But you tried your best. And you failed." She let the word sit there like a judge reading a verdict. "Boldness won in the end. It always does, and now I have my daughter back."

"What makes you so sure?" I still hadn't lost my anger at

nearly being encased in foam at Gemma's orders, but the variable of Chaos was too great to ignore. It had clearly done something to Amaryn. I needed to understand what that was.

"After you left, I was talking to her like I always do, but I could feel a difference. It was like I was connected to her somehow. I whispered in her ear that I just wanted to hear her voice again. I wanted to know she was still with me. That's when the box appeared."

I looked back down at the music box. The porcelain face of the ballerina was intricately detailed, the wood softly finished. Inlaid into the top of the box was the seal of the artist. It wasn't something you could pick up in a hospital gift shop to pass off as a miracle.

"We lost that box years ago, before Amaryn was even a teenager. After I told her I wanted to hear her voice again, it showed up right on that table and started playing. She heard me, Zoe. I asked her for the rocker next. It's the same one my mom used after I was born, and what I used with Amaryn. Look at her now, almost the same age I was at the time. Isn't she gorgeous?"

Gemma brushed a strand of hair away from Amaryn's turbulent red eyes. Under the glow of the streetlight coming through the window, the girl's skin showed webs of veins along her neck and cheeks. The Chaos seemed like the last thing fastening life to limb.

"I tried to bring her back fully, of course, but that hasn't worked yet. Still, Chaos did exactly what I asked it to do—it gave me another chance with my daughter. It's all I ever wanted."

She was out of her mind. "Things like this don't just appear out of nowhere. That's impossible and you know it."

"Of all the people who shouldn't be questioning what Chaos is capable of. With all that snooping around you just did, you should know what it can do."

The fire that had propelled me back to confront her swelled to life. "I was a little busy being shot at."

"You were trying to steal my property, and I will always protect what's mine."

"There were *people* in those cells."

"Whatever they were before, they're monsters now, and I keep monsters locked up."

My voice shook. "Like you kept me locked up?"

She reached over and pulled the blanket up higher across Amaryn's lap, my only answer a wry smile.

I thought I knew better. I thought I'd learned how to spot the lies of someone who only wanted to control me, but here I was again, squarely under the thumb of someone just because they pretended to care. I had an overwhelming urge to hurt Gemma like she'd hurt me, orchestrating pain from behind a mask of kindness. I wanted to take away the upper hand she so comfortably held—to wipe away that infuriating smile. The music box sat only a few inches away. I wrapped my fingers around the brown curls of the dancing figurine and slammed it to the floor. It shattered in a satisfying crash.

The sting of the impact's sound faded to silence while I waited for the satisfaction of her heartbreak. Instead, Gemma scanned the debris like she was bored of its existence.

She leaned down slowly to whisper in Amaryn's ear. As her words passed in a hiss, the air in the room changed abruptly, like a static charge passing through it, vibrating the air in my chest. My skin bristled beneath my clothes. The charge dissipated as soon as Gemma fell silent. She came back up smiling.

The sound of metal gears beginning to turn drew my attention back to the table. Sitting on top once again, the music box resumed its concert, only this time the porcelain dancer was painted a dark golden blonde to look just like me. My mind raced, trying desperately to extrapolate exactly what Amaryn could be capable of. I was too off-balance to concentrate. My own laughing expression mocked with each pirouette of the dancer.

"Go on," she said. She stood and walked behind me.

I followed her over my shoulder. "What are you talking about?"

"Use your power. Tell me what you see."

A battle sparked in my head as I struggled against the urge to defy her, while being all too eager to tense my muscle and escape to the safety of the Silence, and equally as curious to see what waited for me there. I left Gemma's gloating smile behind and turned toward the music box. As my vision divided into repeating segments and the rush of nausea subsided, I was left with an image of the toy stained with Chaos. I could almost hear the energy pulsing through the wood. Marbled red light *moved* through the grains—even though I'd paused the flow of time. I'd never seen anything but myself move through the frozen world before. Something had pierced the silent sanctuary I thought was my own. When I looked over at Amaryn, her eyes were wild red flames, boiling with a ferocious, angry current.

I inched my fingers closer to the music box, hoping to freeze it in time and regain some of what was mine, some semblance of control. Tendrils of smoky flares like the surface of a red sun rippled along the edges. I touched the side of it, ready to flip my mental switch. A shock wave of force pushed my hand away. I lost my grip on the Silence, and the crawling red light disappeared as I came rushing back to reality.

I grabbed the edge of the table to steady myself while I tried to catch my breath.

The figurine danced.

Gemma stepped around me and bent over the box. "What did you see?"

I didn't want to tell her. There was a greediness to her voice like she couldn't wait to use whatever glimpse I could give her into Amaryn's power. "I didn't see anything," I said.

"Nothing? What about Amaryn? Did she look different?"

I shook my head and stayed silent, trying not to think about the girl's violent red stare.

Gemma's eyes dimmed as she stood back up. "You're lying."

"I'm not."

"Yes you are. You're a terrible liar. Tell me what you saw. She's awake, isn't she?"

The greediness was back in her tone. She was right, too. I was a terrible liar, and I was also bad at hiding how I really felt, which kept my anger unmasked when I answered. "She's barely alive, if there's anything left of her at all. You failed."

Gemma gave a short laugh, eyes fixed on me, unblinking. "You are a petty, jealous little creature."

I was done listening to her. I turned to leave. As I walked to the door, I heard the rumbling hisses as she spoke. The air seemed to spark as I grabbed the handle and turned. The door held fast. It was like trying to twist stone.

Amaryn.

"We're not done talking to you," Gemma said.

The room's information screen glowed next to me; its Alarm button plastered in red at the bottom. I tapped it and waited for it to connect.

More of Gemma's hushed instructions filled the room with an electric charge. The room lights blinked before dying out. The info screen spasmed and went black. An emergency light in the corner triggered, shining blood red light onto the empty bed. Alarms blared throughout the building.

Through it all, Amaryn's lifeless stare watched it happen.

Someone in the room below us screamed. Another cried for help. Amaryn wasn't the only one whose life depended on a machine. "Gemma," I said as voices grew in urgency from the surrounding floors. "Turn the power back on."

"My gods, she's amazing." Gemma looked happily around the room, admiring her daughter's work.

People on the floor beneath us were shouting orders. One of them screamed for someone to check the generator. Outside, a crowd of people huddled beneath the roof of the Emergency Ward entrance. The sliding doors were stuck with only an opening too narrow for anyone to fit through. A pair of EMTs banged on the glass with a small girl on a gurney between them.

"Make her turn it back on," I said.

More screams for help drifted up.

"*Now*, Gemma!"

She waited as if she wanted to draw the last bit of thrill from the panic Amaryn had caused. With a performant air of mercy, she bent down to Amaryn's ear again, whispering an order.

The lights in Amaryn's room blinked to life first, followed by a wave of electricity returning to the hospital. One by one, the floors came back to life. *How many people did she just endanger —or kill?* The thought made me sick.

"There," Gemma said, obviously pleased with herself. "See? Like it never happened."

I couldn't believe what I was hearing. "People might've just *died* because of that little stunt. How do you not see how insane this is?"

I'd spoken the words without thinking, forgetting that all it might take would be a few whispered words in Amaryn's ear and it could be the end of me. I thought I saw the faintest hint of a smile on Gemma's face, as though she, too, realized how much power she controlled now.

"Feels like a different world all of a sudden, doesn't it?" she asked. She looked ready to rule this new world. "I knew Chaos could help my little girl, and I was right. You have to admit I was right."

I held back the urge to fight with her, as powerful as it was. As much as I hated to admit it, she held the upper hand. I wasn't getting out unless she let me. "So, what happens now?"

"The work continues," she said. "I want you back at Valhalla to continue your research now that I've made this breakthrough. We should keep trying to understand what Chaos can do. Amaryn isn't quite back to full health yet, but she will be."

Beside her, Amaryn sat propped straight in her rocker, Chaos burning in her eyes.

"I can't just show up to work tomorrow like nothing's happened."

"That's exactly what you're going to do."

"And if I don't?"

Gemma knelt beside Amaryn's chair, stroking the dull gray of her cheeks before looking back at me. "You're a smart girl, Zoe, but you're also insufferably naive, so I'll spell it out for you. This isn't you helping me anymore, this is you *working* for me, and I'm telling you your work isn't done."

"I could go to the World Union," I said, but the threat died a muted death as soon as it left my lips.

Gemma leaned in to whisper into Amaryn's ear, and I braced myself as the charge danced through the room.

The door clicked open behind me.

"You could," she said, "but you won't."

"And why is that?"

"I told you—I keep my monsters locked up, but those monsters can be let free, and if I see so much as a blue and white uniform even approach my tower, I'll see to it that my monsters fulfill their new purpose. And don't think I've forgotten about Britt, either. One word from me and she'll be set loose to finish what she came here to do."

She glared across the room as if daring me to test her resolve. I didn't need to. I knew she meant every word. Now that she'd shed the mask she'd worn to keep me in line, there was no mistaking who Gemma really was and what she was capable of doing.

I also knew what Britt was capable of.

A thought wound itself through my brain, threatening to materialize when it was the last thing I'd ever wanted to consider before. I couldn't help myself. If it came down to it, would I freeze Gemma to save myself? Could I do such a thing?

Maybe.

But there has to be a better way.

I looked at Amaryn, a lifeless weapon of mass destruction, lying in wait like an unexploded bomb and her mother holding the finger on the detonation button. I needed to defuse the bomb if I wasn't willing to kill the person holding the trigger. I still had the pictures of the files I took from Valhalla. I needed to make sense of those first and then figure out a way to get rid of this curse once and for all.

"Alright," I said. "I'll stay."

"At your apartment," she ordered. "You're not welcome back at the lake house."

I nodded even though I had no plans to go back to my apartment, where I assumed she had eyes to watch over me. I needed to find a place to work, somewhere where I could concentrate on deciphering the information in that file.

"Tomorrow marks a new day then," Gemma preened. "For all of us. Now that she's better, I think I'll take Amaryn home. I'll need to fix up her room again." She smiled, lost in thought. "Think of it," she said, dismissing me by returning to stroke the matted hair of her daughter. "The power to shape reality, Zoe. Think of what Amaryn and I can do."

It was hard to think of anything else.

CHAPTER THIRTEEN

MY FIRST ORDER of business after leaving the hospital was to throw the keys to Gemma's truck in a bush and find the nearest rental car place. Given the last twelve hours, I felt justified in my paranoia that the truck was too easy for her to track. My debit card was another easy tracking target, so I got cash out of the bank before heading east. I drained my savings of everything but a couple dollars. After spending most of my money on my escape from La Grange, it was only enough to keep me warm and fed for a couple of days, but it would do. I'd think about a plan for making money again once I'd made sure Chaos couldn't hurt another person.

A car-share place near the hospital had a white electric two-seater available, a common enough car that I would easily blend in with the commuters on my way out of the city. I studied the hotel options along the way, looking for somewhere I could think through my next steps away from Gemma's watch. I finally pulled into a motel halfway up the Cascades near Snoqualmie Pass. I remembered seeing it during the first trip to the cabin. It looked like a place where the beds came with a side of bugs. It also looked like it was easy to ignore, with a staff who wouldn't ask a lot of questions. Exactly what I needed. Minus the bedbugs.

I tried not to think too much about facing life on the run again and instead went over my admittedly light-on-details plan again as I parked the car in a spot near the motel office. Even though I didn't have the whole binder from the Valhalla containment cells, I still had pictures of the first couple pages on my phone. Whatever secrets they held, they were important enough for Gemma to lie about. Anything that valuable had a better chance of helping my search for a cure than a few blank graphs did. I just needed to figure out how to decrypt the gibberish. The good news was that if it did give me a direction to go, I was a walking blood bank for Chaos-tainted samples.

The woman behind the dirty office window checked me in without looking up from her crossword. A thin trail of smoke meandered out of the cigarette she pinched between weathered fingers. I left behind a five-dollar tip because she didn't make me repeat the obviously fake last name I came up with. The room key dangled at the end of a red plastic diamond with the faded motel logo on it. She also handed me a bucket with a plastic liner.

"For ice," she said. She ashed her cigarette. "Free of charge."

The cursed mixture of air freshener and moldy carpets greeted me at the door as soon as I jimmied the room key in the lock. I cracked the lone window and turned on the overhead fan. Even the plain wooden chair at the desk felt like it was coated in a layer of grime. It was a long way from Havenwood.

It's only temporary, I thought. My future seemed to be lining up with temporary situations. Nothing to do except make the best of it.

So, I ordered pizza.

While I feasted on overly greasy pepperoni slices, I sat

down at the desk and flipped through the images I'd taken of the folder. Doing some research on what type of encryption the symbols might represent was the first order of business. I started by searching for the latest trends in data security. Most of what came up in my search had to do with reverse engineering passwords and port attacks on routers. I tried some of the simpler decryption techniques using their built-in code window—and got excited when one of the routines didn't error out immediately—only to come crashing back to earth when the page timed-out with a debugging error.

This is out of my league. The more I stared at the coded lines, the more I wondered how I ever thought I'd figure out what they meant. For all I knew, they were the words to a nursery rhyme. There was no way I was decrypting the sequence on my own.

But maybe I know someone who could.

Anjo.

There was only one other person besides Gemma who had the knowledge to access those files, and that was her second in command. Compared to my failed attempt at codebreaking, pretending to be an intimidating force seemed like a piece of cake. I didn't dare go back to Valhalla, though, where I'd be directly under Gemma's surveillance. I had to get him alone, away from that place, and I had an idea how.

But first I needed to find him.

Getting his last name was easy enough. There weren't too many Anjos that worked at Valhalla and had a networking account with the WU. Finding his socials wasn't much harder, but the only one that wasn't locked down tight was his Nearby dating profile. According to his bio, he was looking for someone that could keep up with his "corporate lifestyle." I couldn't roll my eyes harder. He also listed that he preferred redheads.

I grabbed the keys to the car and shoved down the last bite of pizza on my way out.

Okay, lover boy. One enterprising redhead, coming up.

FAKE PERSONA IN HAND–COMPLETE with an AI image of the woman Anjo was sure to fall in love with—I headed back to Seattle, parking my car a few blocks from Valhalla to grab some much-needed sleep while I waited. Just before lunch, I created Dreamgirl Deborah's profile and set my options to search for anyone within a half-mile radius. It took less than a dozen swipes before I got to Anjo. I marked him as a favorite and sent him a message:

Hey! I'm in town for a long layover and just wondered if you wanted to grab a bite to eat while I'm here?

Classic hookup scenario—or so the internet told me. I'd never been a flirt and definitely never an aggressive flirt. After hitting send, I wanted to shake off the imaginary coat of slime like a dog coming in from the rain. Now I just had to wait for the bait to be taken.

Sure enough, he replied back in less time than it took to bring Dreamgirl Deborah to life: *Yeah, for sure! Meet around noon? I know a place near my flat that would be perfect.*

He ended the message with a wink emoji. I wanted to barf.

Around noon, I pulled my car into the parking lot of the restaurant Anjo suggested. Seeing as this was my first time trying to intimidate someone into giving me information, I wasn't sure if I was supposed to corner him in the building or out in his car. I finally decided that the fewer people who saw my performance, the better, so I left my car running to pull in beside him whenever he showed up. A fashionably late Anjo rolled in almost twenty minutes later driving a dented burgundy sedan that looked like it was on its third engine battery. *How is Deborah ever going to keep up with his corporate lifestyle?*

He parked near the back and promptly started to primp himself in his rearview mirror. I took the space next to him and parked so close that he couldn't open his door. I got out before he could see me, and as he was yelling from inside for me to move my hunk of junk, I grabbed the passenger door handle and slipped inside.

"Hello, Anjo."

He nearly shrieked, barely holding in a squeaking scream. "What the hells?"

"Sorry to interrupt your date."

I caught his glance toward the phone resting on the center console. Before he could make a move, I slipped into the Silence and flipped my internal switch to freeze it in place. When I came back out, he jumped again.

"Shit!" He reached down and tried to pick up the phone, yanking at it twice. "Oh, come on."

"Relax," I said. "I just need to ask you some questions."

He put his face in his hands. "Oh gods, she's going to fire me. Or kill me. Or fire me and kill me."

"Anjo!"

He jolted.

"No one's going to kill you. Gemma doesn't have to know anything if you just stay calm and talk to me."

"Yeah, okay," he snorted. "I'm sure she'll consider this a funny little mishap."

"Will you shut up for a second? I just want to show you something." I pulled out my phone and brought up the images of the files. "You know what this is?"

He squinted. "It's a patient profile. Can I go now?"

"No. I need to know what it says. Why is she keeping this file so secret?"

"It's Ms. Weeks. She keeps everything secret. Anything

kept on paper has to be encrypted. And she's the only one with the key."

Of course she was the only one. "But you've seen what's in here before, right?"

He shrugged.

"Listen," I said, softening my voice, "I'm only trying to help. If there's something in this file that can help me cure what Chaos does, I need to know it. It's more dangerous than we realized. Than she realized. Trust me on this."

"More dangerous than her?" he asked. "I don't think you understand who she really is."

"I'm starting to get an idea."

"If that were true then you wouldn't be here." He leaned his head back against the seat. "You're talking about someone who came up from nothing and took over a billion-dollar company, and she didn't do it by being understanding and kind. She tore through the old bastards who ran Valhalla like they were nothing. That's what made me want to work for her at first, but then I saw what she's capable of. She shows you as soon as she thinks you're a threat to her power—just ask her ex. So no, Zoe, I'm not interested in *helping you*. I'm interested in not dying. I'm way more scared of her than I am of you."

Even when she wasn't in the room, Gemma still managed to control everything. It was infuriating. I tried to regroup. If appealing to Anjo's good nature wasn't going to work, I needed to scare him. And since people were scared of what they didn't understand, it was time to show him what he didn't know about me.

"Do you know what happens when I freeze things?" I asked.

Anjo looked straight ahead without answering.

"I stop time from moving through them. I haven't had to try it on a person yet, but I have a theory on what it would be like—First off, their body would go without oxygen for as long as I decided to keep them frozen. They wouldn't be able to breathe. Their heart wouldn't pump blood. They wouldn't be able to move when I came back into the flow of time, but they'd be able to see me. I would watch as their body shut down, and they wouldn't be able to stop me. And you saw what I did back at Valhalla. I can move without anyone ever seeing me—whether it's across a hall or across a seat." I made a show of shifting toward him. "By the time you notice the light coming over my skin, it's already too late."

His nostrils flared as he continued to stare out the window.

"Whether or not you become my first test subject remains to be seen. So, I'll ask you again," I said. "Whose information is in this?"

"You wouldn't do it."

"Try me." The hardness in my tone wasn't entirely part of the act. I pictured Gemma sitting there in his place—or Britt.

The standoff ended with a slump of his shoulders. "You already know it's an infected. You saw them in Containment."

"I found two of them. There were three folders. Whose is this?"

He looked like he might cry. "Cedric's."

Finally, some luck. The one person Gemma desperately wanted to keep secret. "What does it say about him?"

"I've only seen the unencrypted version once, but it said something about him needing special attention."

I paused. "What kind of special attention?"

"I don't know. Something to do with his reaction to Chaos. He used his power and never came back. Can I go now?"

"Maybe." Being an intimidating force was hard when all I wanted to do was quiz him on the science. "What do you mean he never came back? Where did he go?"

"Mars. The surface of the sun. Beats me. Where do you go when you blip and move?"

"So, you're saying he, what? Disappeared?"

"No, that's why he's under supervision. His body is still

here, but his mind is long gone. Ms. Weeks wants to know the second he wakes up, so she keeps him where she can see him."

"And where is that?"

Anjo shook his head. "Gods, she's going to kill me."

"You can tell her I threatened to turn you into a paperweight. Where is he?"

He answered through a sigh. "The lake house."

I looked straight ahead, trying to make sense of it. I'd been through every room at that place and never saw a thing. "Are you sure he's there?"

"Positive. I sign off on the medical equipment every month."

I must have missed something. But if Gemma thought he was important enough to hide, finding him was my top priority, not to mention getting him away from her clutches.

"Thanks for your help, Anjo."

"You know I still have to call her now, right? I'm dead if I don't."

"Yeah, I know." As much as he annoyed me, I didn't want to subject him to Gemma's wrath. "I'll unfreeze your phone after I'm gone, but you're going to give me a head start first. If I see anyone from Valhalla following me, I'm coming back for you first, and we'll test that theory of mine. Are we clear? Good." I opened the passenger door. "Be sure to tell her hi for me."

"Wait," he called out just as I was about to leave. He leaned across the arm rest. "So, is Deborah, like, a friend of yours or…?"

I shut the door.

My next stop was the lake house. I needed to find Cedric, quickly. Maybe between the two of us we could figure out how to rid the world of Chaos before Gemma burned it down in search of her cure.

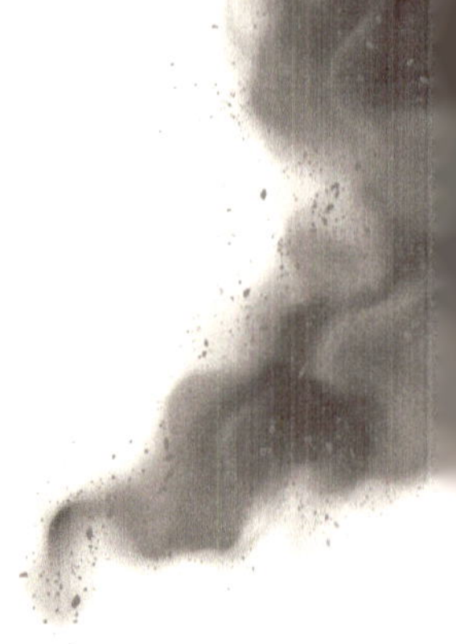

CHAPTER FOURTEEN

THE CABIN LOOKED different as I drove up. After learning that Cedric was somewhere on the property, I saw it in a new light—another puzzle for me to solve. I switched off the car's engine. The cabin was so small, it seemed impossible that I could've missed him inside. The only other structure was the barn where the truck had been, so I headed off to check it.

There was enough afternoon sun coming through the gaps in the wood that I could see my way through the stacks of hay left to mold over the winters. I walked every inch of the building, coming away with nothing but stains on my shoes from the muddy floor. I checked the backyard next. No doors leading to a cellar or even so much as a crawlspace for tools. The only interesting find in the scrub of trees behind the property was an empty soda bottle whose glass was milky from age.

With nowhere else to check except the bottom of the lake, I walked back into the cabin. There were only four rooms to check beyond the living room—two bedrooms, a bathroom, and the kitchen. My search didn't take long. I even looked under rugs in both bedrooms, hoping to find some secret entrance to a basement. All I found was an old felt bookmark, so tattered and worn it might've been Gemma's from when she was a girl.

It was hard to imagine Gemma as anything but a commanding woman hells-bent on conquering the unconquerable. I couldn't picture her resembling anything as normal as a young kid reading a book.

I dusted myself off after searching beneath the couch and started to wander, scanning with hands on my hips to find *something* that might give me a clue. Standing in the hall, I noticed once again the framed portraits leading from the living room down to the bedrooms. For the first time, I noticed a picture of Amaryn. She was by herself at the edge of the lake, sitting cross-legged in a patch of yellow wildflowers. Her smile was barely noticeable, a tilt at one corner of her mouth like it's all she could muster when she was ordered to smile. She looked like she was maybe year ten, the same age I was when my mom gave me bangs for the first time. It made me look like a much younger kid. Maybe that was the point. I wondered if parents did stuff like that to hold on to the image of the child who'd never leave their side. Past the sullen facade of a pre-teen were eyes that couldn't hide the hope she seemed to have. The luxury of innocence. I decided on the spot that if I couldn't save her, I'd try to see to it she was in a place where she'd been happy once. The girl deserved at least that.

Going from one picture to the other was like seeing a family tree grow right in front of me. Gemma's red hair went back four generations. It might've been more, but it was hard to tell when the images became black and white. I studied the picture of Gemma as a child. A woman who must have been her mother held her hand. She had Gemma's thin nose in addition to her red hair. Another woman, the matriarch of the family, held arms around them both. The grandmother smiled proudly, the satisfied look of someone secure in the knowledge that her dynasty would continue.

Barely visible against the backdrop of trees was the fishing pole in Gemma's hand.

Seeing the image reminded me of one more place I hadn't checked. Gemma mentioned that her mom kept fishing supplies in the little hall closet. I turned and squinted in the dim light to see the lines of the door, hidden within the rest of the wooden slats. The pull handle wouldn't budge, locked in place.

I dug through every room in the house searching for a key. The lock was so ancient, I wondered if the key wouldn't look like one of the old skeleton keys from the movies, but there wasn't so much as a bobby pin in the cabin. I rifled through the main bedroom's desk. I tossed all the drawers. Nothing.

All my power and I couldn't break into an ancient lock.

Maybe I can freeze it.

I grabbed what I needed—some duct tape, a straw from the kitchen, and a can of compressed air I saw on the desk in Gemma's room. If my high school Chemistry teacher could've seen me, I don't know if she would've been proud or embarrassed at what she had wrought.

After going back to get some water in a cup, I covered the keyhole halfway with a piece of tape and slowly started to fill the cavity with water, inching the tape up the entire time so it wouldn't let any out. Once I'd filled as much as I could, I sealed the keyhole the rest of the way. Then, using the thin nozzle on the compressed air, I punctured the tape and pressed the trigger. The air coming out of the nozzle was so cold, it only took a few seconds to freeze the water-filled cavity.

The mechanism inside snapped, splintering the old wood around it. A couple of hard pulls and the lock came free.

"A-*gods-damned*-plus, Zoe Daniel."

The door came open easily, releasing a breeze of stale air. I held my breath through the brunt of it, amplifying the sound of blood rushing in my ears. I waited impatiently for my eyes to adjust.

The tiny room was filled with fishing equipment, as advertised, strewn across the floor like a forgotten game of pick-up sticks. It was too dark to know for sure, but the door was about half the size of the height inside the closet, extending five or six feet on either side of the opening. I felt around for a light switch and found one just inside the door on the right. A single fluorescent bulb flickered on. I stuck my head inside.

In the light, I could see another rectangular outline on the ceiling of the closet, along with a knotted pull string. It looked like it was done as a weekend DIY project—hand-cut lines with a cheap piece of board acting as the door. Despite knowing it could be another dead end, I couldn't help but feel that I'd finally found what Gemma was trying so hard to hide.

I pulled the string , ready to enter the Silence if I needed to.

The door creaked open to reveal a metal ladder leading to an attic. A thin cloud of dust showered down on the rungs.

This is it. My hands were almost too shaky to keep hold of the ladder's narrow steps. The air became hot and stagnant as I climbed to the top of the ladder. A high pitched whine sounded as soon as I stuck my head above the mouth of the attic door. A single red light flashed on the face of a small metal housing. *Motion detector.* I entered the Silence and froze the device, putting an end to its high whine, but it was probably too late. Gemma would know where I was. Electricity swelled in my chest. If Cedric was here, I needed to find him quickly.

Clutter filled the attic space from the plywood-covered beams on the floor to the rafters. A jagged path created by stacks of musty cardboard boxes wove away from the makeshift door and then cut right. Everything about the attic was stale and ancient, a decaying snapshot of a world left behind. Even the sound of my footsteps seemed muted, like I was on the doorstep of the Silence. I paused with each step, straining to pick up even the slightest noise. My ears hummed with tension. I turned the corner and stifled a scream.

A man stared back at me from the end of the row, sitting in an old wooden rocker with a faded blue hospital gown draped over his gaunt frame. A tattered afghan covered his legs. His eyes were as bright as bulbs, beaming with intense red light. The surface of his eyes reminded me of the sample of Chaos I first saw in the lab, writhing against its glass cage. They cast a red glow over his overgrown beard, which stuck out from his cheeks and chin like a wild thicket. He had a head full of dark curls that had somehow not grown over his face, like someone had been cutting it short to keep it out of his eyes.

"Are you Cedric?" I asked.

My words died gently in the hollowed space.

I took a quiet step. "What happened to you?"

The man held his silent pose, still as stone.

I walked toward him, slowly making my way through the stacks of boxes. He didn't move, not even to breathe. His skin was pallid, as if he'd been covered in a layer of dust along with everything else in the attic. As morbid a thought as it was, the absence of the smell of decay was the only thing keeping me from assuming he was dead. Just because he wasn't decaying didn't mean he lacked a stench. I stopped when I was within arm's length, waving the air in front of my face to interrupt the rising musk from his afghan. For a second, I wondered if he'd been frozen in the Silence. It was how I imagined a person might look if I doomed them to that fate.

Whether he was stuck in the void in between time or not, one thing was clear—he was another victim of Chaos.

I touched his hand, hoping it might stir him out of his catatonic state. His skin was cold and paper-thin. Checking his pulse was like pressing against a raw steak, but his heart still beat in rhythm, if only weakly. I wondered how long it had been since he'd eaten anything, or even had fluids in his body. Mine were the only set of footprints in the dust. I checked around for an IV drip, but there was nothing. He was a living corpse seemingly trapped by Chaos—and maybe kept alive by it. Most of his fingernails were dark and overgrown. Others had fallen off completely. The hem of his scrub's inseam seemed to be stained with mold.

"My name is Zoe," I said. "I'm here to help."

It was hard to be close to him. The penetrating smell of his unwashed skin burned my nose and throat. I stood up to clear my head. I had to get him out of the house. Where we went from there, I had no clue, but I couldn't leave him in the rocking chair another day to atrophy.

The thought occurred to me that I could call the World Union.

I imagined what that road could lead to—the resources of Valhalla versus the global authority of the WU, with me and Cedric in the middle. It wasn't a position I was eager to be in. For either of our sakes.

Something to my right moved.

Startled, I pivoted to see an old kids' chalkboard easel leaned against the wall next to Cedric. "Amaryn" was spelled out in magnetic letters along the bottom. The face of it had long-faded drawings of a cloudy sky. Then, as I watched, the drawings started to disappear. The chalk began to wipe away in white streaks, like something was erasing it with an invisible hand.

Or someone.

"Cedric, are you doing this?" I asked.

There was a moment of quiet before letters started to appear on the easel. The unseen chalk scratched against it as it drew out the words.

GET OUT OF MY HOUSE

I pushed down the urge to do just that. I couldn't run. There had to be an explanation.

Cedric watched on, silently.

"I'm only here to help," I said.

LEAVE ZOE

"Gemma?" It seemed impossible that she could be doing this, but also it felt right.

The letters started to scrape furiously onto the board, erasing themselves as quickly as I could read them.

NOW BEFORE I HAVE YOU TAKEN OUT

YOU WONT GET ANOTHER WARNING

I took the easel and dropped it to the floor before she could threaten me again. The clock was now ticking. Whatever I was going to do, it was time to do it.

I turned back to Cedric to try to piece together my next move. I couldn't leave him there, not after seeing the state Chaos—and Gemma—had left him in.

Before I could figure out a way to get him to the car, I heard footsteps on the gravel outside. I hurried down to the other end of the attic where I could look out through a vent in the side wall. Two jet-black Valhalla Security cruisers sat parked on the side of the house. Four guards—each carrying spray fire neural weapons—descended on the front porch.

"Gods damn you, Gemma."

The cabin door crashed open downstairs like it had been kicked. I ran to the attic door and pulled the ladder up. The guards rushed to the noise. I flexed and entered the Silence to freeze the door in place.

Once I touched my finger to the plywood and felt the familiar pinch of cold as I switched it off, I turned my segmented gaze toward Cedric's chair. His body was gone, replaced by a doorway that stood where I expected him to be. It looked like someone had cut a rectangle out of the air between his empty chair and the attic wall. Hazy shapes drifted across the front of the doorway like mud-colored clouds, unaffected by the hold of the Silence. I had to spend precious moments of safety trying to make sense of what I was seeing. I'd gotten so accustomed to the world around me forced into silence by my power, and now this was yet another violation of its law, just as the music box was—another variant of Chaos that existed beyond my control.

I could only hold my muscle flexed for another second. I wanted to see more. Beyond the man, another world potentially teemed with life and maybe a promise of safety.

I let go of the Silence. As soon as I rejoined the flow of time, the footsteps of the guards came to a stop beneath the attic door. They tried once to break their way through, a vicious rap against the handle with what sounded like the butt end of their guns. The frozen door would've sooner snapped their guns in half. Safe for the moment, I turned my attention back to Cedric, who still sat in his chair outside the Silence. The doorway to the other world was gone. I ran over to grab him so we could try to escape through the vent on the other side. Halfway through the path of boxes, the wood splintered ahead of my step as a spray of neural charges shot through the wood.

I stumbled at the sound. Pieces of the attic floor lay scattered on the path. One more shot like that and the guards would have a way through.

Downstairs, the guards cocked their guns again. I had to move. Without wasting another second, I flexed, let the yellow light wash over my skin, and entered the Silence to make my way past the opening.

The doorway showed itself once more, only now it was just a few feet away, beckoning. My Silence was a pocket universe where nothing penetrated the slices of time, not even sound, but with the doorway's appearance came a vibration almost like electricity that sent unnerving pulses through my body.

The opening was only a few painful steps in front of me. I could make it without time walking. I took two steps and braced myself against the building pressure. The surface was tantalizingly close. I reached my hand to it and pushed my fingers through before I could think of the thousand different reasons why I shouldn't. It was like dipping my hand in bath water. The other side felt warm against my skin. Through the membrane, my hand appeared blurred and dull, but intact.

I took the last painful step through to the other side.

Warm air filled my lungs. I drank it in thirstily, my body spent by traversing the Silence. At the same time, my eyes tried to absorb everything at once. I was on a boardwalk near a busy oceanfront beach. People milled around me in steady streams. As much as I'd been forced to consider the impossible over the past few weeks, even this seemed surreal. I almost touched a woman as she passed by just to see if she was actually there. The air smelled thick with brine. For some reason, the way people dressed stood out to me more than the fact that I was somehow back outside, miles from where I'd entered the Silence. It was the fabric. Almost everyone wore shorts that glistened like early morning sunlight on the water. I'd never seen anything like it, yet there was hardly a single person who didn't have their bodies covered in the shimmering cloth.

I turned back to the doorway. Above the entrance, a hand-painted sign read, "CEDRIC'S, est." and then a smattering of chipped paint where the year had faded out. There was no hazy image of Gemma's attic waiting for me on the other side of the door. No guards bearing down on me. I'd escaped—but to where?

I felt a sudden need to sit down. I began to make my way through the flow of people. Eventually, I found a bench ahead of me. A man sat on one side, reading a paperback with one leg lazily draped over the other. His hair somehow held its shape against the steady coastal wind. The curls seemed instantly familiar. He lowered his book when I got close and greeted me with a genuine smile.

"Hey, hey, look who it is," Cedric said, tucking his book away. "What's shakin', Wraith?"

CHAPTER FIFTEEN

I FUMBLED FOR WORDS. "What did you call me?"

"Let's start over. I'm Cedric, just like the sign says," the man replied, pointing to the store behind me where I'd emerged from Gemma's attic. He held out his hand for me to shake. "And you are Wraith."

"It's Zoe," I said. "Where are we?"

He motioned for me to take a seat, and I was happy to get off my wavering legs. A man raced past us on a longboard that didn't have any wheels. The Space Needle was still on the northern edge of downtown, but the spire was different— shorter. The ferries were painted blue along the bottom instead of green. A woman in glistening running shorts passed by. I stole another glance at the bizarre fabric. Everything about the world around me was unsettling, like it was just slightly *wrong*.

Cedric smiled. "I like your hair this way. Usually, it's up in a bun all the time. I think it makes you look like a Sunday school teacher, but what do I know?"

"How could you know what my hair usually looks like? I just moved to Seattle."

"Ah! I see." He took out a pen and made a note in the book he carried.

"What are you doing?"

He clicked his pen. "Sorry. Bad habit, but if I don't write it down I'll forget. We should probably start from the beginning. That usually works best for us. I'm Cedric."

"I know. I came here—"

"And you always say, 'I came here to help you' when I repeat my name the second time."

It took a wide section of my hair rippling across my eyes from the ocean breeze before I blinked. A semester of Theoretical Physics in college had prepared me for a lot of things I told my professor I'd never use. It was possible I was about to owe him an apology.

"Is this another version of our world?" I asked, looking around again at the sights that felt nearly familiar.

"Fantastic!" he said, clapping a hand on his knee. He clicked his pen and made another note in his book. "Fastest time yet, and Wraith 34 was pretty fucking fast. Do you think my clue was too on the nose? I probably gave it away. I need to work on that. You're getting an asterisk."

"What do you mean *34*, and why do you keep calling me that?"

"What?"

"Wraith."

"Because you are the…," he trailed off to check his notes. When he looked down, I could see the red Chaos in his eyes reflecting off the sunglasses he used to hide his condition. "Yeah, you are the four hundred and fifty-first version of you that I've met. Sometimes you're just Zoe, like today, and other times you're already Wraith, like you're going to be after you go back."

Clearly, Chaos had not done Cedric's brain any favors. "I'll be Zoe when I go back. No one calls me that."

"I think it changes from world to world, but generally it's

the press who gives you the name. Trust me. You have other names too, but I stopped writing them down because they were stupid."

Four hundred and fifty-one versions. Me, copied across universes like the infinite split slices of time in the Silence. I could hardly fathom that parallel worlds were real. This was a man who, in my universe, was a husk of a human that Chaos had given the ability to experience these theoretical worlds somehow.

"Hello? Zoe? You still with us?"

"Sorry, this is a lot to take in, and to be honest, I'm starting to wonder if I hit my head back there."

"Take your time. But not too much time. I like to hit the library after I talk to you."

I sat back on the bench to face the stream of people walking along the boardwalk. Before Chaos, I never would have believed it was possible to walk through an invisible doorway to another universe. I still wasn't sure I believed it, but the list of things I thought I knew grew smaller by the second.

"What year is this?" I asked.

Cedric bobbed his head from side to side like he was trying to loosen the fact from memory. "This version of good ol' Earth is a little different from the rest. They counted all the years in between Ancient Earth and New Earth, so to them it's 1.2M45k—one million, two hundred thousand and forty-five. To you and me, that's just 2045, but 2045 in the reality you and I came from is just a bit behind, if you haven't noticed. These shorts are sweet, huh?" He pointed at a man jogging past. "That *very fabulous* fabric powers all of their wearables— immersion tech, tracker shoes, you name it. Incredible. Hard to go to the bathroom in though. Also expensive as shit. Did you know they don't have pennies here?"

I turned to face him again. "So, you were exposed to Chaos, and now you're stuck traveling through different universes. Or are they traveling to you? I've seen your body back in our reality. It's not in great shape. You don't have much time to stay here, I'm guessing."

"Time!" He laughed like I'd just delivered the punchline to an hour-long joke. "I'd forgotten people cared about that. Yeah, to be honest, I'm not worried."

"You should be. I'm not an MD, but your body looks like it's getting close to shutting down."

"Oh, I'm pretty sure that happened a long time ago." He closed his notebook and smiled like a teacher about to address the first day of class. "Let me guess, I was super skinny, pale, skin kind of loose and nasty, long-ass beard. Sound about right?"

I nodded.

"That's what I looked like a year ago when I first walked out of my store there, carrying a history book I'd found inside. You may not be the stethoscope-slinging kind of doctor, Zoe, but I'm pretty sure you know what would happen if I went a year without eating food or drinking." He feigned a gagging choke and flopped dramatically. "Deadzo. But, thanks to the miracles of Chaos, I'm here. For now. As soon as you leave, I'll head back into my store and pick up another history book to head somewhere else. See how this works?"

Hardly. "Don't you want to go home?" I asked.

"Home? Hell no. I hated that place. Plus, I owed child support there."

His frantic laugh left me uneasy. Time might not mean anything to him anymore, but it was obviously taking a toll on his psyche. I looked back through the tide of people to the store. I couldn't see past the shop's opening. The darkness of its shadows made me wonder if there was anything still there for me to go back to. My breath froze in my chest. "Wait, you're talking in past tense. Are you saying we're stuck here?"

"I was wondering when you'd get to that. Let me put that little stress ball you have for a heart at ease; you ain't stuck here. Whatever's going on back through that red door will still be waiting for you when you return."

Something *was* waiting for me back through the door. I was in no hurry to face it, but I couldn't ignore it either. "When I go back, you and I will both be in danger. Gemma—"

"Ah, come on. Can we not talk about her? Kills the vibe."

"I'm not going to stay here. I can't. She's—"

"Ugh!" he interrupted. "Vibe-killer alert! *Again*. You have about two seconds to become interesting, or I'm waltzing. Zero stars. Wraith 362 was way better."

It was like talking to a teenager who'd magically become an adult for the day. I needed some answers. Maybe if I played his game, he'd give them to me. "Fine. What else is in that book shop of yours?"

"Mostly boring stuff, but there's always a history book waiting for me. My favorite kind, as it turns out. Ticket to sometime, somewhere. It doesn't matter how shitty a version of Earth I end up in either, I can always find the book I need to keep going."

I couldn't help the swell of questions building inside, even though I needed to steer the conversation back to Gemma and Chaos. "Do you always go forward in time?" I asked.

"Nope, although I stand out less in the future."

"Do you get to choose where you go?"

He watched the crowd as he answered. "As soon as I find the right book—meaning the next version of the history book I've already written in—I open it to the new blank page for my notes, and then I always end up right here when I leave the shop. Permanent Seattle resident—just don't know who the current mayor is, if you know what I mean. Could be worse, though, right? I mean, this could've happened in L.A." He shuddered.

"So how far back have you gone?"

"Let's see…" He pretended to think while a smile spread

across his face. "Do you have any questions about *archaeopteryx*?"

I stared at him, waiting for the punchline while he beamed. "Is that a dinosaur or…?"

"Is that a—? Of course, it's a dinosaur! My god, I thought you went to school, Zoe."

"Not to be a paleontologist, asshole, and it's Dr. Zoe to you." I tried to steer the conversation back to Chaos, no matter how much I suddenly wanted to quiz him on whether triceratops really fought T-Rexes. "Am I the only other person you've seen multiple times?"

"The only Chaotic? No. The only Chaotic I want to talk to multiple times? Yes."

Even though I knew there were others, it was deflating to know Chaos had spread in multiple timelines. I was losing hope for the world waiting for me back in the store. It was time for Cedric to give up the answers I came looking for.

"You call us Chaotics."

"I call most of you pieces of shit. You included, sometimes."

"Then if you've talked to me before, I've probably told you that I want to cure this disease. Chaos is too dangerous to let free. Have you ever spoken to a version of me that's solved it?"

He looked like a parent forced to tell their child for the first time that Santa didn't exist. "No, but I tend to meet you early on. Who knows what kind of award-winning science you get up to later!"

"But you've seen other futures where it still exists."

He see-sawed his head again. "It's tough. This isn't Chaos's first rodeo, you know. All those stories about ancient Earth that talked about the little girl who basically wrecked all our supposed gods? She'd totally mainlined Chaos since birth. Hells, our little red cloud friend has been to the center of the universe and back. So, what I'm saying is, maybe dial back those goals some."

Not likely. "I can still cure it," I said. "It's not too late."

He smiled as the wind tugged at his curls. "I do admire your confidence. And hey, maybe I'm wrong, huh? After all, I've never seen your particular future."

I had to focus on my world, not the worlds upon worlds Cedric was forced to visit. "Come back with me," I said.

"Hah! No."

"Cedric, we can stop this. I need to study how Chaos affected you. How it's affected me. There's an answer to this problem, and it starts with understanding how it works."

"What, you want me to be your guinea pig? Poke me with some needles while you sit behind a microscope? As fun as that sounds, Doc, I'll pass. Chaos is the best thing that's ever happened to me, or did you miss the part where I told you I've seen dinosaurs?"

"It's too dangerous."

"Oxygen is dangerous, Zoe. Ask any fire. That blue stuff up on the moon that everyone on this planet is killing themselves to get? Twice as dangerous and ten times as plentiful. There's no putting the genie back in the bottle—kinda literally—so instead of fighting it, just…" He lifted his nose into the air and took a dramatic deep breath. "Relax."

"Relax." I held the comment in my head for a moment and tasted the audacity of it. Not everyone got free multiversal travel out of the deal. Amaryn was back through that doorway being used as a wish machine by her mother.

I reached up to take off his sunglasses.

"Hey!"

With his face now exposed for everyone to see, a chorus of gasps and shrieks spread from the people passing by. Cedric's glowing red eyes blazed. He snatched the glasses out of my hand and fumbled to get them back over his eyes quickly.

"The hell, Zoe?"

I pointed to the people still gawking over their shoulders at us. "Put yourself in their shoes. What do you think they're gonna do when they find out there's people like me who can stop time, or people like you who can walk between worlds. They're going to start an arms race, and Chaotics will be forced to fight. No matter how that ends, it doesn't end well."

"You're telling *me* how things end? Trust me, I've seen a lot of shit, and I'll continue my bookstore universe hop, thank you very much. It's safer this way."

I felt like a lifeguard trying to save a drowning victim who liked the taste of water. I decided to try one last tactic. "And do you ever stop to think about the effect you're having on these worlds?"

"You mean like when someone takes off my glasses to make sure I leave a mark?" He pushed his rims up the bridge of his nose with his middle finger.

"The butterfly effect is an exaggeration," I said, "but the principle is sound. You could be doing real harm here and not know it."

"What's the alternative? I go back with you and slip back into that rotting zombie that's left of me? I haven't felt this alive in years. I'll take whatever rain I cause in Lima if it means I get to spend eternity traveling to infinite worlds. Clear? Good." He clicked his pen and opened his notebook to jot down a note.

"What are you writing this time? That my sixtieth appeal to your humanity failed?"

He snorted. "Just making sure I remember things. Sometimes we meet again. I like to check on your progress when we do."

Starting to think I don't want to meet you again. With Cedric's refusal, I was back to figuring out how to deal with the police Gemma ordered Amaryn to send after us. My eyes settled on the door to CEDRIC'S once again.

Cedric shifted closer. "What's your plan?"

"I'm not interested in filling more entries in your notebook, Cedric."

"Okay, okay. I won't write anything down, I promise. Just hit me."

I sat back and tried to put my jumbled thoughts together. "Honestly, I don't know. I know I have to go back. I know I can't do nothing. But what happens if I fail? What happens if I don't cure it?"

Cedric sighed. "I know you don't want to hear this, but you might need Chaos, Zoe. Not every day that's coming is a good one."

"What do you mean by that?"

"I'm just saying, maybe you got Chaos for a reason. There are people that will need Wraith one day."

"That sounds ominous."

"That's the one downside to all this," he said, gesturing to the alternate version of Seattle. "Sometimes seeing how things turn out is a real downer. This power you've got, though. It can make a difference. You and your friends will need it."

"Friends? Not sure I remember what they are."

He snorted. "Well, they're more like work acquaintances if you must know."

"Thanks, Cedric."

"There's always another option," he said. "You could run."

It was impossible to know if he was pushing buttons he knew were there or if he'd just happened to offer me the one thing I always seemed too ready to take. "Isn't that what you're doing?"

"One hundred percent. And proud of it, by the way. Like I said, I wouldn't go back to that shriveled body bag for all the money in the world. As far as I'm concerned, what Gemma did to me was a gift."

Did? The word struck like a hammer. "Gemma told me you were exposed by accident."

He scoffed. "It was no accident. Have you ever been kidnapped before? It's not like you slip and fall and whoops you're a science experiment. She takes people off the streets. One night. you're sound asleep in a Seattle halfway house and the next you're pumped full of magical mystery juice in a windowless room. I was scared shitless when they took me—until, that is, I started reading my books."

A well of gravity formed in my stomach. Gemma had been infecting people with Chaos, maybe killing them in the process. "How many others?"

"Let's just say I wasn't the only poor soul forced to stay in Hotel Gemma. I was, I think, the first one to survive, though. After Gemma found out what Chaos gave me, she became really sweet. Motherly, even. All I had to do was submit to more tests so she could find a cure for her daughter."

"Amaryn."

"Yeah, that was her name! Poor little tax deduction. When I told Gemma I was all done getting pricked with needles, she turned to threats. Said I'd be locked in a cell for the rest of my life. I invited her to eat a plate of shit. I was the one with the power, and it wasn't just my new history books. Her husband came to see me, all curious about what her new project was. I told him everything. Dumb bastard went straight to the WU and blew the whistle—on his own wife! That's cold. Her solution was to have her goons move me somewhere the WU couldn't find. I escaped to my bookstore to get away from whatever tortures she planned for me. Best move I ever made."

No wonder Gemma had him tucked away in her attic. He was a loose end, and the one thing I'd learned about Gemma was she couldn't stand someone she wasn't able to control.

"How is Amaryn?" Cedric asked. He pulled out his notebook again and flipped through some pages. "Worm food yet?"

"Gemma gave her Chaos," I replied. "It didn't help."

"But that doesn't mean it didn't have an effect, right?"

His smile was knowing. "This has happened before?"

"Plenty of times, according to all the other yous. Spoiler alert—she's toast."

I didn't want to accept it. "She's still alive, and that means she can be helped."

"You *sure* she's alive?"

I hesitated. "I saw her."

"You saw what Gemma wanted you to see. Amaryn is dead, and Gemma knows it. She's off her rocker, Zoe. But you knew that already. She thinks Chaos can bring her back, but it never does. If someone could just convince her of that, it would save a lot of people in a lot of universes a *whole* lot of trouble."

Dead? "But I…I saw Amaryn use Chaos. I saw what she can do."

"Was it her doing that, or was it her mother? Because universes come and go, but the one thing that never changes in this book"—he tapped his notebook—"is that Chaos doesn't give Amaryn powers. It gives them to Gemma, and she won't quit trying to find a way to make Chaos bring her daughter back."

"No…" I didn't want it to be true, but everything he said fit with what I'd seen. Amaryn's body looked like it was close to decay when I saw her in that rocking chair. Gemma could have easily been infected when she gave Chaos to Amaryn, though, just as easily as I had been.

A nightmare scenario started to form in my head. If Amaryn truly was dead, then Gemma was sure to find out which of them had the power, if she didn't know already. I couldn't imagine her having the ability to affect reality the way she had so far. If she could create a world of her design just by whispering in someone's ear, it wasn't just me or Cedric who was in danger. She wouldn't stop until she had her daughter back. She would infect the world if she had to.

I wasn't going to let that happen.

I stood up.

"Leaving so soon? You haven't even tried the fried blueberries yet."

"I have to go," I said. "I'll come back for you when it's safe."

For all his manic bluster, a moment of calm seemed to wash over Cedric. "Don't. I'm serious. You've got more important work to do, Zoe. If you're really gonna try to stop Chaos, it sounds like you still have time. But not a lot. Don't waste it trying to help me. And hey, if you ever need me again, you know where to find me." He smiled. "Just not *when*."

We parted with a silent nod. I made my way through the people on the boardwalk, never taking my eye off Cedric's store. Gemma's obsession with Chaos had to be stopped before it infected more innocents, and I was the only one who could do it.

I let my fingers rest on the bookstore handle. I looked back at Cedric. He raised a hand and smiled, his image disappearing behind a river of people.

I turned back and stepped through the doorway, back to face what waited in my world.

THE SMELL of wet cinders hit my nose before the first raindrops could. I let go of my hold on the Silence as soon as I stepped through the door between worlds. For a moment, I wondered if I was still in Cedric's alternate universe when I got to the other side. The sky was a blanket of inky clouds bleeding moonlight through cracks in the storm. Fat drops of water smacked against my skin, matting my hair in seconds. Instead of walking out into Gemma's attic, I stood in the smoldering remains of her house with Cedric's decrepit body crumpled on the ground at my feet, naked except for the remnants of his charred robe. His eyes still glowed red. The fires had spared him, somehow.

It hadn't spared the guards. Their bodies had been reduced to melted husks dotting the remnants of the house.

Part of me still wanted to believe Gemma wouldn't resort to murder just to protect her control of Chaos, but the truth stood scattered around my feet, a slick sheen of rain over torched remains. Whatever questions I had about how far Gemma would go had been answered in blood.

She hadn't hesitated.

Would I?

CHAPTER SIXTEEN

I REACHED DOWN and grabbed Cedric by the arm, slinging it over my shoulder to pick him out of the debris. He was as light as a bird. I stepped through burnt bits of flooring and shattered picture frames on my way to the barn, the glow from his eyes lighting our way through the sheets of night rain. The barn had been far enough away to escape the blaze. I propped Cedric up against a turned-over wheelbarrow, naked and dripping rain from his ragged beard, but otherwise no worse for wear. I covered him with a tarp I found on a shelf to help keep him dry. His Chaos-covered eyes stared unblinking toward the open barn door.

I thought back to the moment when I tried to freeze the music box Gemma controlled and couldn't. I wondered if Gemma had tried to have us killed outright in the blaze, and Chaos prevented it in a weird sort of self-preservation. If that was true, she'd probably set the house on fire to see if it would kill us indirectly once she knew the guards had failed. Being in Cedric's world may have saved us. The realization made me cold despite being out of the rain. Gradually, though, a rising heat replaced the chill. Gemma had tried to kill me. I wouldn't let her have a second chance.

"You're safe here," I said to Cedric, even though I knew he was worlds away. "I'll come back for you. I promise."

After I'd dealt with Gemma.

I walked out the back of the barn and into the darkness of the storm. The rain hardly registered anymore as I trekked down the gravel driveway to my car. The drive would give me time to figure out exactly how I was going to stop Gemma.

While I walked, I asked myself if I could use my power on her if it came down to it, and I knew my answer immediately. I would absolutely freeze her to stop the spread of Chaos. If she died because of it, I'd pay the price. It was worth it not to live in a world where unchecked Chaos threatened us all. The only question was whether my Chaos would let me do it.

The rain dissipated once I got to the highway. Specks of moonlight filtered through the clouds, reflecting glints on the gravel to guide my way. My eyes stayed focused on the lights of Seattle in the distance as I drove through Snoqualmie Pass, visible each time we crested a hill. I half expected the city to be floating in air guarded by dragons, but it was ominously still, a layer of low clouds casting the tops of the skyscrapers in a haze.

I pulled my car into a lot just a few blocks from Valhalla. The black tower was nearly invisible set against the night sky. Only a few lights were on. I eventually came to the same intersection where I'd paused on my way to the first interview with Gemma. My misophonia was in overdrive from nervousness back then. Now it was back. I could hear every squelch of rubber tires on the pavement, but I kept my earbuds in my pocket. As much I wanted them, I needed to be alert.

I rounded the corner toward Valhalla Tower and immediately stopped when I heard a scream echo down the narrow, empty street. A man sped around the corner and rushed past me, looking over his shoulder every few feet. I started to jog toward the building. Then, as I heard more people yelling from the direction of Valhalla, my jog turned into a sprint.

A security guard tumbled out of the revolving front door, barely able to gain his footing as he scrambled away. His hat rolled into the gutter as he took off down the street. Another guard and a pair of Valhalla lab workers came next. Last out the door was the woman I recognized as the Valhalla receptionist.

I grabbed her arm to steady her as she nearly fell trying to figure out where to run.

"What's going on?" I asked.

Her wide eyes looked straight at me and yet I didn't think she registered who I was at first. Then I saw the recognition briefly beneath the frantic, scared flits of her eyes. "Gods, not you, too."

"What are you talking about? What's happening in there?"

Her voice shuddered. "She set them loose."

"Set who loose?"

"The Chaotics."

She jerked her arm free and sped off to join the rest of the crowd fleeing the tower.

Chaotics. My whole body felt electric at the unwelcome reality of having to face someone like me. It might not have to be a fight, I told myself. Whatever Gemma had done to them, I could help them deal with it or help them hide from Valhalla. I could get them away from Gemma's clutches to a place they felt safe.

Sirens wailed in the distance on all sides. Whether it was local police or the WU, they wouldn't be able to help. They'd be in just as much danger as anyone else if I didn't find the Chaotics first.

I fought my way through a swarm of people pushing through the revolving doors. Broken windows littered the floor around the entrance. A chair lay beneath a layer of splintered glass. Information screens around the reception desk blared static. Lights flickered. It looked like the aftermath of an earthquake. People fought to get down the stairs from the open second floor, including a man in a security uniform who pushed a woman out of the way, pursued by someone half his size. They sprinted down the stairs after him like a lion chasing its prey. The guard rounded the corner at the bottom of the stairs. Just as he was about to pass the front desk, his foot caught the edge of the counter, and he went sprawling to the ground, giving me my first real glimpse of the person behind him.

There's one.

Their face looked like an unfinished painting, features misshapen and muddled with one eye larger and higher on the cheek than the other. Their hair was a ragged combination of long black curls and short brown tufts. A single breast pushed against the smaller shirt on one side, while the other side of their chest laid flat. They eyed the man scrambling on the floor at their feet, sizing him up and looking increasingly as if they were about to pounce.

"Don't!" I yelled out.

I couldn't get across the lobby in time to shield him, even if I'd time-walked. The Chaotic jumped into the air like they were about to dive into a swimming pool and then landed on top of him, arms spread wide. Instead of hitting him, the person melted through his uniform, leaving behind the naked body of a woman. Her torso sloughed off the guard's chest, lifeless.

The guard rose from the floor just as I ran to his side. He stood, slightly taller than he had been, the muscles of his chest and arms rearranging in front of my eyes like two people fighting to fit inside his skin. This time his eyes looked like they were sliding off his face to either side. His nose nearly fell into his mouth. Wild streaks of brown hair stuck out like seeds on a strawberry next to the guard's red hair.

"This isn't your fault," I said as the haphazard stare of the guard settled on me. "You're infected with Chaos. If you let me, I can help you."

"We don't need *help*." It was like listening to a room full of people answer at the same time.

Another group of screams sounded, this time from the bank of elevators. Two cleaning workers burst out of the stairwell door, looking over their shoulders as they stumbled into the lobby. One of them shouted that a monster was coming. Just then, a pair of arms and legs that looked like they were made of star fields appeared through the closed metal door. The door melted into their skin, disappearing into the reddish-orange outline of the man looking like a window into space. The door was gone, drained from existence simply by coming into contact with the man's body, like starlight emptying into a black hole.

He stood in the middle of the bank of elevators, taking tiny steps toward the lobby with his arms testing the air in front of him as if he had no eyes to see.

Gods, Gemma, what have you done?

"That one," the Chaotic who inhabited the guard slurred, turning the more protruded of its two eyes toward an athletic blonde trying frantically to dial out on the security guard's phone. "We will be pretty *and* strong."

I stepped in front of them. "Don't do this."

The human amalgam recoiled, looking momentarily shocked that I would interfere, but the surprise quickly gave way to anger. They grabbed my sleeve and tossed me through the air like swatting away a fly. I only had a second to see where I was going before I entered the Silence, my head mere inches away from slamming into the floor.

I'd only ever entered the Silence while standing, but when the nausea faded, I was horizontal, staring at the floor. I twisted and reached with my hands as if I was trying to steer myself in outer space until I finally touched the ground again. The effort took too much out of me, and I had a sudden need to let go of my hold, but before I did, I turned my segmented gaze to catch a glimpse of the Chaotic who threw me. They appeared as a small girl wrapped in the red light of Chaos, maybe a middle school kid by her size, and she was as skinny as a stick. The image quickly transformed back into the grotesque as I lost my grip on time. I had to throw out a hand to catch myself against the side of the lobby desk as I came to a sliding stop.

While the star field man ambled aimlessly to my left, the girl's avatar sprinted toward me with massive fists raised above her head, ready to squash me like a bug. I grabbed the first thing I could—a trucker hat left behind on the floor—and held it out like a shield, flexing to freeze it in place just as their clasped hands rushed toward my head. Their fists crashed into the weave of the hat. Finger bones snapped against the surface.

Indignant, furious eyes flicked toward me. I flexed again while she shrieked in pain and switched the hat off again, only surfacing from my pause long enough to grab the hat and move it in front of her avatar's face. Another flex, another freeze, and she rushed head-first into the brim, knocking her back against the desk hard enough to send her crashing to the floor.

I switched the hat off again while she writhed on the carpet. I didn't want to kill the girl inhabiting her victim's bodies; I wanted to help her. But I couldn't let her go.

I placed the hat on top of her face and froze it.

"You bitch!" she screamed through the mesh. "I'll kill you! Take it off!"

I looked around at the people still in the building, searching for Security. A few of the guards huddled meekly nearby, carrying neural guns at their side like the impotent weapons they now were. "Do you have zip ties?" I asked them.

One of the men nodded. He took out a handful and walked them over to me slowly with one arm extended like he was holding a steak out to a hungry lion. He dropped them at my feet and rushed back to the others.

"Nobody go near this one," I said as I looped a pair of the ties together and bound the amalgam's hands and feet. If I had to freeze something else later, the ties would keep her from hurting others. "I'll come back for her when I'm done."

The girl—still masquerading beneath her victims' skin—struggled angrily against the mesh and foam anchor keeping her in place.

I turned my attention to the walking star field, who continued to wander blindly around the lobby. As he passed by the bench near the elevators, I saw his reflection in the metal legs. His shorts and shoes were clearly visible despite the field of stars moving across his body. Whatever Chaos had done to him, it was a veneer, a deadly costume that seemed to absorb anything he touched.

"Can you hear me?" I called out to him.

His head turned toward me, searching for my voice. "Who are you? Where?"

"I'm a few steps in front of you. Just follow my voice."

With no expression except the void of space to look at, I couldn't get a read on him. His attention wavered between me and the frantic shouts of the people still fleeing the building. He nearly came into contact with a man running past him. I stepped in to guide the runner out of his way.

"I don't know where I am," the star field man said.

"It's okay. I'm here to help. What's your name?"

He seemed lost, pausing to answer like he hadn't thought of himself as someone with a name. "They kept calling me the Void, but I… My name was Samuel. *Is* Samuel."

"Then Samuel, I want you to walk toward my voice. I need to get you away from these people. Do you know what happens when someone touches you?"

He paused, then nodded his head. "I think so."

I didn't need to ask for details, no matter how much my

curiosity begged me to. I could hear in the withering inflection of his voice that something terrible waited for whoever was unlucky enough to touch him.

"Alright, Samuel. I'm gonna get you out of here."

"I can't."

"Yes, you can."

"You don't understand."

"I'm a Chaotic, like you," I said. The words fit more naturally than I expected. "I understand better than anybody. My name is Zoe."

Samuel stopped moving and turned his head in the direction of my voice. He no longer seemed lost. Even without a face, I could sense the predatory stare. "Could you say that again?"

Something wet tapped the skin of my arm as I tried to silently back away from him. His head twitched from side to side, searching for my footsteps. Between us, something like rain started to fall. I glanced up quickly to see if perhaps a third Chaotic was causing it. Another drop hit my cheek. I rubbed it away and looked at my hand. A crimson viscous liquid glazed my fingertips.

Chaos.

The drops came faster, confusing Samuel's frantic search. The few people left in the lobby ran for cover. Outside, a man screamed that blood was falling from the sky. I ran to the window. Beyond the glass walls of the Valhalla Tower, red drops speckled the sidewalk. The clouds overhead roiled in red mist, sending Chaos down in a driving rain. A scarlet bolt of lightning lit the downpour, showing the thunderheads covering the length of the city. There were thousands of unknowingly exposed people already. How soon until that became tens of thousands?

I flinched when I saw Samuel nearby, narrowly avoiding his outstretched hand. Thunder shook the floor beneath my feet. I backed away from his swinging arms as the Chaos rained inside and out, trying to decide what to do in the face of something so overwhelmingly impossible.

I entered the Silence to look for the source of the storm.

From one slice of time to the next, I was surrounded by a static cage of Chaos rain. To my left, Samuel appeared as his normal self, a boney middle-aged man with a sagging belly. His eyes were gone, replaced by red ink wells of Chaos. Behind me, the girl still lay trapped beneath my frozen hat.

I couldn't move, no matter how hard I tried to squeeze through the curtains of droplets keeping me in place. Beyond the walls of the Valhalla tower, innocent people were being infected. Even if only a fraction of them showed signs of abilities, the world would be irreparably changed. Like any virus, Chaos just wanted to spread, and it would leave a trail of dead in its wake. It was already a disaster. I had to stop it before it got worse.

My gut told me Gemma was still in the building, forty floors above with the best view in the house. If she was there, I would do what I had to do to stop her. If she wasn't, I would take every bit of information she'd hidden up in the labs and find a way to cure this threatening plague on my own.

I left the Silence to see Samuel still waving his arms through the rain to find me. I backed away from him and shouted through the storm. "Stay here! I'll be back."

He spun to face me, still desperately searching. "No! Come back here! *She won't let me free if you run!*"

Now it was clear—Gemma put out a bounty for my head and released her test rats to collect. I understood her thinking in a twisted way. I was the only person who could potentially ruin her plan.

I tried the bank of elevators first. A pair of digital zeroes blinked above each one. I put my hand to the Valhalla scanner and it flashed red. *Locked out.* With the steady rain of Chaos soaking into my hair and clothes, I ran to the stairwell. The rain continued inside, streaming through the flights of stairs like they weren't there. I readied myself for whatever might be waiting for me at the top while I climbed. Gemma had already sent her bounty hunters after me. I doubted she'd just let me walk through the door once I got there.

I slowed as I approached the final set of stairs to the fortieth floor, sweat mixing with rain and my legs burning from exhaustion. The downpour stopped as soon as I cleared the last flight. The walls of the landing ran red with shadows of the Chaos storm still raging outside the windows.

And then in the doorway, Anjo stood underneath the lab entrance sign. A metal ring surrounded his neck. His hands and feet were bound in chains that wrapped around his body and connected the metal neck ring to the sides of the doorway. Sitting in the middle of his bound hands was a digital timer attached to something that looked like a plastic explosive. The numbers 0:01 stood on screen.

Anjo's eyes pleaded with me as he struggled to breathe beneath the chains bound tightly over his mouth.

"You're going to be all right," I said. "I'm going to make sure that doesn't go off."

He shook his head violently.

I took a step toward him. The timer came to life, marking its march toward zero with a shrill chime. I flexed immediately, and once the rush of nausea passed, I saw a pair of small motion sensors sitting on either side of my feet, their invisible tripwire now sprung. Anjo sat frozen mid-thrash against his chains.

The timer sat at the edge of my limit, paused with only a few tenths of a second left. If I left the Silence, even to go right back in, there wouldn't be time to save either one of us.

I had to move. Pain swelling with each step, I pushed myself across the gap. The strain lit my muscles on fire. Each step weakened my grip on time. I was close to passing out near the end. I couldn't go any further, and as I reached out into the slices of my vision, the tip of my finger brushed against the edge of the explosive. As soon as I felt the flash of cold that told me it was taken out of time, I let go of my flex and collapsed at Anjo's feet.

His cheeks were coated in panicked tears, his eyes bloodshot. Slowly, his breaths shallowed as he searched himself as though he couldn't believe he was still alive.

The display sat frozen mid-transformation into a zero.

"We're okay now," I told him, trying to catch my breath.

His entire body quaked. He nodded, still crying.

I pointed to the bomb. "This can't go off anymore. You're safe now. I won't let her hurt you."

As soon as I said the words, I took a look at the unguarded open door behind me and realized what Gemma had done. She knew I could only freeze one thing at a time. If I tried to use my power to stop her now, Anjo would die.

Gods damn you, Gemma Weeks.

The bonds holding Anjo in place were too intricate and too strong for me to break without using the Silence in some way. He closed his eyes and shook his head. He looked resigned again, like whatever I meant to do was doomed to fail. Maybe it was, but I had to try.

I walked past him, steadying myself to enter into the labs once again.

The darkened office held an odd murmur, like an echo of the people who once filled it with noise. There was just enough light making it through the storm outside to cast the sea of gray desks in speckled red streaks. I pictured Gemma back in her office watching her daughter's bastardization of reality. I'd check for her there first. I felt the tremor of each step, ready to flex at a moment's notice. There was no telling what Amaryn could conjure anymore. If she had limits, I didn't know them.

Without my ability to freeze anything, I needed a different weapon. I picked up the only thing I could find—a sharpened letter opener from one of the desks. I could use it if I had to

—anything to keep Gemma from whispering in Amaryn's ear.

It felt like a different person's thoughts flowing through my mind. But Gemma was endangering others. Thousands were already infected. This wasn't me, but it was the person I had to be—for now.

Gemma's office light broke the darkness near the end of the lab hallway. I turned the letter opener, gripping its handle, until its blade rested against the inside of my arm. I walked through, ready to do what needed to be done. As soon as I stepped around the threshold, an ancient plywood staircase greeted me in a dark cinderblock room lined with shelves filled with tools and paint cans. I caught my breath at the sight. I had to blink and rub my eyes to make sure I was seeing it, but the room that had been her office was now something that looked like the basement of an old house. If she wanted to unsettle me, it was working. My arms and legs trembled. I was walking through a world that shouldn't be. It was a trap, but it was a trap I had no choice but to spring if I wanted to find her.

I started up the wooden stairs. Through a doorway at the top, I found myself in a large country kitchen that opened up to a living room filled with faded beige couches and a burgundy love seat. It was something straight out of an old farmhouse, and it was all cast in a sheen of red from the windows. In the center of the room, Amaryn lay in the same rocker I'd seen her in at the hospital. Chaos still pulsed in her eyes. A pair of pillows hugged her emaciated body, now covered in a yellow flowered dress. Her matted hair had a blue ribbon in it.

"You've done some remodeling," I said, doing my best to give off a sense of calm.

"This is the house we lived in when Amaryn was a girl. She grew up in it. I wanted her to see it when she comes back to me." Gemma was calm, like she, too, was back home where she wanted to be. She sat beside Amaryn sipping coffee from a ceramic mug. She stayed close enough to her to speak her whispers if she needed to. "I take it you ran into Anjo on your way in. I wanted to make sure we could talk in peace without worrying about which of us could outdo the other."

"Gemma, look at what you've done. Those people out there are terrified, and most of them are going to end up in a coma from exposure—or worse. You have to stop this."

She scoffed. "Put the genie back in the bottle, you mean? You know as well as I do that's not possible. And why would I? Look at what *is* possible." She beamed proudly at the windows and the crimson world outside.

"You're forcing this on people who didn't sign up to be science experiments, and for what? The off chance that one of them can bring Amaryn back?"

"Yes," she said. "Most of them will stay the way they are, true. Boring. Forgettable. But some—some will show how *special* they are. If all goes well—if this works as I assume it will—then Amaryn and I will be together again. If it doesn't, we'll continue our project."

"What project?"

She looked out the window. "We've started small. For now, only those people outside will get the chance to realize their potential. After a few days, we'll see who rises to the top and what they can do."

"This is crazy."

"No, it's the science you were hired to do. I wanted you to get control of this, but you failed, and now Amaryn is running out of time. You've given me no choice. If only five percent of these people exhibit abilities, one of them could use Chaos to bring my Amaryn back."

I looked at Amaryn's body slumped awkwardly in her chair. Cedric was right. She was already gone. "And if they can't, what then?"

"Then we strengthen the storm."

That was it. I didn't need to hear anymore. A world full of Chaotics would lead to nothing but its namesake.

I moved a few steps closer to her. Her cup shattered as she rushed to Amaryn's side. I wanted her to have that confidence that she could stop me. I needed her to stay in place so I could reach her.

"Zoe, before you take another step—"

I moved forward, ready to enter the Silence to take the last few steps before she could react.

"You should know something."

I stopped only a few feet away, well within range to put an end to her terror. "I already know. I know Amaryn is gone. I know the Chaos worked on you."

Gemma relaxed her shoulders. "Cedric…," she said through a sigh.

I turned the letter opener until I felt the blade against my fingers and tensed my grip, ready to strike.

"I suppose you know all my secrets then," she said. "Save for one."

A stinging pain radiated across the back of my neck. I dropped my weapon, suddenly unable to make my fingers work well enough to hold it. Rivers of cold electricity flowed down my extremities, taking my energy with it.

"Anjo will be let go," she said as a haze started to swallow my thoughts. "I promise you that. I'm afraid I can't say the same for you, though."

I turned around, fighting to regain control of my body. I fell to my knees. My vision dimmed, but not before I saw the needle that punctured me, and the woman holding it.

"Hello, Zoe," Britt said. Her orange prison uniform filled my fading sight. "I missed you."

CHAPTER SEVENTEEN

THE SMELL of pine trees lit a spark that briefly pierced the darkness of sleep. I remembered the scent vividly. My parents took me on a car trip up the Pacific coast for my high school graduation present. We were trying to make it to Evergreen by dinner, but my father didn't account for traffic getting out of San Francisco and my mother was so mad she wouldn't speak to him. The car was painfully silent. I was too afraid to say anything, so I put the back window down and hoped neither of them would make me put it back up. They were too busy being mad to care. I closed my eyes to try to get some sleep with the cool air of the Cascadia Forest brushing over my face. As I drifted off, I could smell the faint scent of pines in the northern Cascades. I'd only read about them in books before, but I remembered how energizing it was to smell something that made me feel so clean and alive. All I wanted was to hold on to that feeling now that it was back. I didn't want to wake up to lose it.

Open your eyes, Zoe.

Unwelcome consciousness rolled in like a creeping fog, and with it, the gradual recollection of what had happened. Bits of memories bounced off each other, sometimes connecting like a puzzle. Amaryn. Valhalla. My escape across country. A new life. Chaos. Gemma.

Britt.

She was in prison. Had she really escaped?

I opened my eyes, too afraid to wonder whether Britt was real or not. I needed to know.

Britt sat in the darkness of her car, surrounded by the din of tires on blacktop, eyes fixed forward, her features lit by the dashboard display.

As I pieced together more of my surroundings, I looked down to see my hands bound together, palms facing each other with fingers wrapped in tape. Thick ropes wrapped my ankles, thighs, and torso. The rigid angle of my body agitated another memory of Britt adjusting the seat on our first date so I would sit up straighter. It made me prettier somehow.

The little hatchback lurched over a pothole. I slid from left to right, unbuckled, and hit the side of my head on the window.

"You're finally awake," Britt said. She smiled as she turned to me. It was the smile of someone who looked as though they'd just won a marathon—spent, yet full of victorious pride.

"Where are you taking me?"

"Hm. Somewhere I think you'll like."

Her bundle of keys clinked against each other after another bump. The sound scraped claws across my nerves. I shut my eyes. She'd always kept a long chain full of useless keys on rings. I hated it when she drove, and she insisted on being the one to drive anywhere. The random clinking of metal, never in the same pattern, brought my misophonia back in an overwhelming wave.

"The woman back there—the one you tried to replace me with—said to make sure your hands were taped," Britt said, nodding to gun metal strips of adhesive around my fingers. "She said those tricks you pulled to get away in the hotel were because you could use your hands. I don't understand the science stuff you do, but I know that'll be the last time you ever run out on me again."

She patted my immobile thigh.

The keys swung wildly as the car hit another pothole.

Wherever we were, there was no Chaos storm overhead anymore. Maybe we were too far away, or maybe Gemma had already found what she was looking for. "Are you taking me back to La Grange?" I asked.

She smiled at me again—knowing, content, tired. "No, not back there. Although we were happy then, weren't we? Before you abandoned what we built. I wanted what comes next to be on my terms. Our terms. I've been thinking about this for a long time."

"Thinking about what?"

"How we die."

My heart clamored against my chest restraints. I wanted to believe I was still unconscious and that all of this was a product of my drugged mind. I didn't recognize the vacant stare she wore or the tranquil demeanor. I'd never seen this side of her anger. Not even when she came through the house full of thunder, searching for me because she was convinced I was cheating on her. Not when she came bursting through the door of the hotel in Seattle. All of that had been exactly who Britt was. This person—the person driving us through the dead of night—was like a shadow of her. An uncaring, unfeeling shadow. I don't think I'd ever been so frightened of what she might do.

"I don't pretend to understand what's wrong with you now," she said. "Or what that Gemma woman can do. None of it matters to me. All that matters is that we're together again."

She turned the car down another unlit road. Tires crackled over gravel. Her keys bounced, strengthening the storm of random, spiking noise.

"I didn't think it would happen this soon, Zo, but you've changed, and that forced my hand. In a way, I'm grateful. This would've been a much longer trip if we'd started in La Grange."

"Where are we going?"

"Let's see if you can guess." She rolled down the already-cracked window on my side. The sound of tires crunching across gravel tripled. Coupled with the keys, it was hard to focus my mind on anything but the rising anxiety brought on by the noise. I tried to breathe my way through it. I needed to be calm to figure my way out. I craned my head as much as I could to let the wind rush over me. Pine scent, earthy and sharp, filled my nose.

"Somewhere in the mountains," I guessed.

"Close." She almost looked wistful. "Don't you remember our first date?"

It seemed like a lifetime ago. One of the nights I wanted to forget more than anything. I should've seen all of this coming. I knew what she was then, and I went along with it anyway.

"Zo?" She put her hand on my thigh and squeezed.

I tried moving my legs to the side, but I couldn't get away from her touch. "Stop calling me that."

"My, my. Look at you. Only a month away and you've lost those Southern manners."

I closed my eyes and went back to lifting my nose into the wind. It was hard to make out anything but the smell of trees, but there was something else there. A small sting against the sweetness.

"I proposed to you that first night," she said.

"I remember."

Britt snorted. "You had the cutest look on your face. You were so scared to answer. I think it was because you knew we were destined to be together."

The shame of not seeing her for what she was then came

rushing back up from its burial in my memories. "I should've listened to myself. I should've known what you'd turn into."

"Hush. That's not you." She squeezed my thigh again, harder this time, before putting her hand back on the wheel. "That night, we talked about where we wanted things to end up."

I wanted to ignore the scene my mind was all too eager to replay. I couldn't help picturing it, though, the two of us at a late-night diner after watching two movies back-to-back. I was hopeful to have finally found someone after so many failed connections before her. She seemed like an almost perfect fit, but even then, even after a few hours with her, I could see the truth of who she was. See it, but not acknowledge it. When we sat down to eat, she ordered my beer for me, telling me she "liked me as a stout girl." Given that I was a few pounds heavier than I wanted to be at the time, I instantly felt hurt, and yet I couldn't figure out if she'd done it on purpose. That unsettling feeling—not knowing if she was being intentionally cruel or not—would stick around for years.

"You didn't go back to sleep, did you?" she asked.

I pulled myself out of the daydream. If I was going to figure out how to survive, I had to focus on her game. "Just remembering that night," I answered.

"So then you know where we wanted to live out our last days."

"No." It was the truth. I only remembered thinking how odd it was for someone in their late twenties to talk about a place to die.

"Well. It'll be a surprise then."

I had to get free. I frantically mined my brain for a way out, some plan to get me out of the car and free of my restraints. I tried to separate my hands in the darkness while Britt's vacant smile was pointed toward the road. The tape was too tight. I couldn't get any room to move.

I didn't want to accept that I was helpless after all I'd been through. I couldn't be. Finally, I braced myself to enter the Silence. The rush of nausea ended with a static view of my prison.

As much as I tried, I couldn't move out of my bindings. My hands stayed in my lap. My legs couldn't move. My arms were pinned to the sides of my chest. The only thing I could move was my head. I turned away from the image of Britt driving, suspended in time, and immediately found my face only inches away from the passenger window.

I was close enough to touch it.

Maybe I didn't need my hands after all. Maybe all I needed was some part of myself to touch something so I could switch it off.

I knew I only had a few more seconds of hold before I had to let go. Assuming I could take the car out of time, what would that accomplish? Freezing a speeding car would just mean that I would be thrown into the windshield. We'd both be dead.

I thought about time-walking. I knew I could leave and enter the Silence in a fraction of a second. What if I did the same thing while bound? Even if I was thrown out of my seat, I could probably reach some part of the car to turn it back on again.

It was a long shot, but it was all I could think of as my hold on the Silence trembled.

I faced the narrow strip of interior fabric next to the seatbelt and strained to make contact with it. With a final stretch, I felt the rough surface against the skin of my nose.

The mental switch never materialized. All I felt was the dull surface of an inert weapon.

I let go of my hold and let the nausea wash over me. The grating sound of Britt's jingling keys dragged me back into the flow of time.

Her eyes stayed trained on the road. "That flash of yours," she said. "What's it do?"

Without the touch of my hands, my power was useless. I stared at the floor. "Nothing."

The car hit another pothole, and my head swung back and forth before knocking against the window. I winced at the spike of pain.

"I guess she was right then, about your hands I mean. I can see why you tried to leave me for her. She's strong."

"I didn't leave you for her," I replied, head still leaning against the window and the breeze coming through it. "You're an obsessive, violent, gaslighting psychopath. *That's* why I left you."

"You don't really believe that."

"There's nothing to believe. You prove me right at every turn."

I'd never been so honest with her or maybe even myself. What did I have to lose? Bound and headed toward whatever end she had planned for me left me without the usual shackles of fear.

Britt sighed through her nose, a sure sign that she was losing patience with me. "All I do—all I've ever done—has been for us, and you still treat me like a punching bag."

"I'm not the one who's been punching all these years. Or maybe you forgot the morning when you broke a rib because I made fun of you?"

"You never let me live that down. I didn't mean to push you that hard, and it's nothing compared to losing my job because you followed Mommy's orders and filed a report."

"No," I said. "I won't let you turn this around on me. Not anymore. I've lived with your bullshit for too long. You're an evil fucking bitch; and if you died right now, no one would miss you, especially me."

I held my breath, waiting for her storm to finally appear.

Britt stared silently, barely moving her hands to steer the car. The fire of her anger stayed hidden, replaced by something that felt even more frightening—detachment.

I could sense the end coming soon, the culmination of whatever sick plan she'd laid out for us. My heart started beating faster. I tried again to free my hands, even if it was just to free a part of my fingers. I didn't try to hide it anymore. I thrashed sideways, hoping I could find something on the door to rip the tape off me.

"Almost there," she said dully. The keys knocked against each other, scraping metal against metal. The sound tore at my ears.

"No, not like this," I said, eyes searching the midnight scene ahead. This couldn't be the end. There had to be some way.

She turned toward me slowly, the dead stare still cemented in her expression. The car lurched as it ran slightly off the road. She didn't look back to correct it.

"I told you I wanted to take you where we said we'd take our next step." Her words were nearly a shout as the car thrashed ahead.

My body swung back and forth as we bounced over the terrain.

The keys' chorus stabbed at my ears.

"We said we'd end our life at the ocean," she continued. She took her hands off the wheel. The engine roared as she pushed the accelerator to the floor.

I looked out at the car's headlights, flashing wildly over rocks and dirt. Beyond the edge of the lights, the horizon stood draped in black.

"And now we'll die there together."

The edge of a cliff entered the field of her headlights, the maw of the ocean waiting.

"Britt, *NO*—"

The front of the car slammed into a rock at the cliff's edge, twisting and tipping it to one side, momentum carrying the back end into the air. With no seatbelt to restrain me, my body rocketed out of the seat and into the side window. My shoulder broke through the glass. Along with a rush of pain, the bindings around my chest loosened, cut by the broken window. My arms were free, but not my hands.

Britt's wild laughter rose above the frenzy of the crash.

And then we were in free fall.

CHAPTER EIGHTEEN

STREAKS OF NIGHT sky mixed with blurred glimpses of water flashed by the windshield as we plummeted toward the ocean. I screamed until my throat felt like it had been sliced into pieces by the broken glass. I was forced to face the fact that my life was at an end. Everything was about to end.

Britt shrieked fits of laughter from her seat.

I should've been preparing to die, and all I could think about was how it didn't seem possible that I could. I was still a part of this world. Still capable of doing something.

Still a Chaotic.

I flexed my internal muscle and got swept into the Silence just as the hood of the car made impact. The static scene almost shocked me into letting go of my hold. Black waves stood ready, frozen in their rush through the windshield to crush us both. Tendrils of water broke through the glass like fingers prying open a door. If I'd waited even a split-second longer, the impact would have killed me. Still, I had a small window if I wanted to survive, even though it grew smaller by the moment.

The force of the twisting fall had thrown me to the back of the car. My shoulder rested on a thin stream of water that had rushed in the rear windshield. There was a gaping hole in passenger side window from my earlier impact. It was maybe wide enough for me to get through, but only just enough. A sinking realization chipped away at my resolve—I would have to time walk to get back to the front seat to escape. The window was too far away to reach in one trip to the Silence. With the car already frozen mid-impact, there were only fractions of a second left before the ocean swallowed us whole.

With my hands and legs still bound but my arms no longer strapped to my chest, I sat up and inched my way back toward the front seats. Britt's hand gripped the leather arm rest in the middle like a child riding a roller coaster. It took twice as much energy for me to move while bound. I felt my grasp on the Silence weakening just as I was almost to my seat. My elbow slipped off the edge of the middle console. I lost hold of my flex and got swept back into time. I flexed back into the Silence as fast as I could, but not before the ocean forced its way further past the car's windshield. During the slip, Britt's laughter pierced my head with a stabbing edge of insanity. It followed me back into the soundless void as an echo in my mind, a reverberating rebuke of my escape.

My stumble cost me valuable space in the cabin. Water was fully through the windshield now, almost as far as the front window. Using only my elbows and knees, I wedged my right arm into the head rest and pushed myself forward, fumbling my way despite the pain as I inched further from where I'd entered the Silence. I could only barely make it past the wall of water inside, struggling to find purchase on the fine ridges of the wave until I squeezed past like I was forcing myself through a crowd. The time walk had already taken its toll. I was too tired to make it out of the car and needed to extend my walk if I wanted to get out the window. I relaxed and flexed as quickly as I could once more. This time the impact of the water drowned out Britt's cackling screams. I still had a ways to go to make it through the broken pane of glass. Getting past it to a safe distance would be the furthest I'd ever moved by at least a few feet, but I couldn't risk another blink. Even a fraction of a second spent outside the Silence and the car would be submerged.

Pain and pressure mounted until it felt like my eyes would burst and my muscles were being ripped apart by glass claws. I could just get the crook of one arm outside the window. I used it like a grappling hook, pulling my body through the opening. Just touching the edges of the broken window elicited a scream that died immediately in the silent void. I held on for as long as I could, but the pain was too much. Before I was forced to let go of the Silence, I got a final glimpse of Britt. Her neck muscles stood on end, her head thrown back in a triumphant roar.

I left the Silence with the image of her imminent death blurring back into reality.

Still in agony, I came back to a world ready to inflict more pain. My time walk might have gotten me free of the car, but the momentum I had before going into the Silence stuck with me, and the impact of the water slammed me backward into the side of the car. My head bounced off the frame. The world went from a melee of thrashing noise to a muted, monotone rush of turbid water as the suction created by the sinking car pulled me under the surface. I sank into the black depths without taking a full breath first. I couldn't tell which direction was up, and I could sense the surface getting farther away with each pounding heartbeat in my head. I entered the Silence, hoping to give myself time to think, even though I knew I'd be the one frozen in place with the water all around me.

Sure enough, the water acted like a tomb, trapping me in stasis. I was too exhausted from my time walk to think my way around the roadblock fast enough. I couldn't muster the strength to hold on to the flex. I had to let go of the only lifeline I had left.

Re-entering time brought back the blazing ache of my lungs as I held my last bit of breath in a vice grip. I thrashed my still-bound hands in a direction I hoped was up. I hit the hood of the car. The weight of the slowly sinking vehicle drove me down further. I tried as hard as I could to free myself from the maelstrom sucking me toward the bottom, but the little energy I had was quickly giving out. I couldn't do it anymore. I couldn't make my muscles move, and the force of the sinking car kept erasing any progress I made, pulling my body deeper into the black.

I entered the Silence one final time.

Like before, I was entombed by the immovable ocean, unable to see or move. The Silence wouldn't be able to save me. The only thing my hands could touch were themselves. So much time worrying about what effect my touch would have on other people and the final object I could freeze was myself.

Britt had won. She'd gotten her wish. We would die as she'd always imagined, joined in one last moment of agony. Maybe it was the anger of giving her the final satisfaction that made me do it. Maybe it was a final attempt at being able to control something in my life. Either way, as soon as the thought of freezing myself entered my mind, I knew I was going to do it. I would go out on my terms. I had no more energy to hold onto my flex, and there was nothing but death on the other side.

I concentrated on my hands pressed against each other and felt the familiar mental switch waiting for my command. In the end, I screamed.

SUCCUMBING to death was like being unplugged, feeling in one moment that you were part of everything in the world and then in an instant, nothing. My field of vision transformed from the bubble of time outside the sinking car to a rush of elongated colorful streaks, an encroaching darkness leeching their hue as they thinned. I waited for the tunnel of streaks to end, to leave me in the void, to lose everything that was myself. All I could do was watch and wait for the end to come.

The tunnel ended in an explosion of yellow light. A staggering vision came into focus, so immense that I gasped with breath I no longer needed to take and cried out with a voice I no longer had. There was no connection to my body at all. The only thing left were my thoughts, and I held on to them fiercely. They were my only connection to my life before, but in the face of visual stimuli so overwhelming, nothing in those thoughts could draw a comparison to what I now saw.

Countless sets of time slices like I'd seen in the Silence filled the golden backdrop. Center slices, larger than the rest, tapered in size until they met the next sections in front and behind them. Layers upon layers of diamond-shaped segments linked together, top and bottom, side to side, creating a mesh of…what? Instances of time? I could barely comprehend it all, and yet I had no physical outlet to work my way through it. From where I now existed, I could see the moment where I froze time in myself. It stood in front of me like a slide of film in the middle of the other slides that made up the last second of my life. Without a way to physically move, it seemed like I changed direction in space by will alone. I shifted to the side, giving myself a view of the complete set of slides, suspended like still lifes hanging in a museum. I saw Britt only inches away from impact with the ocean. I saw shards of glass mixing with droplets of water. I saw pieces of the car's frame already starting to buckle from the crash. And there, in the center of it all, a hazy colorless silhouette.

That's me. That's where I used to exist.

Everything else in the scene was full of color and life. My

remnant was a smudge, an unfinished attempt to erase me from existence. A blank cutout of time I used to inhabit.

Used to. I had no idea if I was dead or alive. Caught in the fabric of time, I felt like an outsider to everything, nothing more than a wisp of consciousness floating through a tapestry of moments. The longer I thought about it, the more intimidating it felt. If this was the fabric of time, I had unraveled it. *Me.* I instantly felt the weight of the enormous power I held, and now it was up to me to determine which way that weight shifted. Despite the strangeness of it all, I felt safe in this space detached from the world. Being an outsider had always felt safe. I had the sense that I could stay amidst the fabric as long as I wanted. I didn't feel the pull of time edging me closer to a breaking point where I'd have to release its flow. That flow was now stopped.

For everyone and everything.

Every second I took to weigh my choices felt like a second I was stealing from the people whose timeline I'd halted. They wouldn't know it, but I would. Even if I could re-enter where my negative self now lay, I might not be able to stop time again before I died. For me, my place in the fabric of time could be at an end. It didn't seem survivable. Still, my life wasn't worth the theft of countless other lives. That didn't mean I wanted mine any less though. I couldn't physically cry anymore, but I felt the tug of sadness all the same. If it came to sacrificing whatever this new existence was so the rest of the world could move on, I would do it, but I wanted to at least try to find a way to join them.

Moments. It's how I started to think of the connected diamond-shaped pieces of time. These moments surrounded me on all sides, all connected through pinpoint slices of time. I eyed some of the ones closest to me, black with turbid water. Who was to say I had to re-enter the moment where I left? I started to move higher, away from the imminent crash. The higher I went, the thinner my consciousness felt, like I was losing myself along the way. It became harder to think, and to remember, as if my memories were tied to the spot where I left time. I stopped climbing before I got too threadbare. This was just like the Silence, only my confinement was even smaller. I moved back down, then left and right to test my boundaries. No matter what direction I chose, the sensation was the same. I was bound to an area, but at least I could move.

I picked a moment a few up from mine, not too far to make me stretch my limit, but far enough to get me out of danger if I could figure out a way to insert myself back in time. From my new position, I'd be near the water's surface. I moved closer to the slices of time in front of me, unsure of just how I would re-enter. I hoped I would feel the tug of time just like I did when I touched an object in the Silence. But I had no hands to reach out, no fingers to press against the slice. Instead, I moved forward until it looked like I was about to break the plane. I could go no further, and yet there was something like a distant echo of the feeling I was looking for, the sensation that I could manipulate time's flow. I moved down the line of shrinking slices. As I went, a sensation almost like a magnet being drawn to its polar opposite grew stronger until I reached the pinching nexus between two moments. This was my doorway back in—I could feel it beckoning. I pushed myself forward.

My re-entry into the flow of time came with no nausea, no feeling like I was rushing through a vortex. Instead, it was like walking into the middle of a silent film. I was surrounded by ocean water, a few feet above my still-frozen body. With the flow of time restarted, I watched as Britt's car careened off my immovable frame on its way to the ocean floor. The car disappeared into the darkness, swallowed by the depths.

She was gone.

I stared at the black depths until I convinced myself that her death was real. Britt was no more.

Was I?

I could move myself through the water just as I did while drifting in the fabric of time, but something was different. I felt somewhat more whole, like I used to feel when I entered the Silence. I held up a hand, shimmering in the water with a warm glow. The water moved around it, flowing over my ethereal skin. I could touch again. I swished my fingers around to make sure the water reacted to my touch—and it did. I held up the other hand, then looked down at the entirety of my body, a translucent figure of light, and then to the body I'd frozen in time below me, still mired in darkness like a sinking statue. I moved like I imagined flying would be, side to side, up and down, untethered by gravity. I was a ghost, moving through the world.

I didn't want to accept that this was my future. Seeing my body frozen in the moonlit depths, I wanted nothing more than to be back in it. My touch had taken me out of time. Maybe now that I had a new body to work with, my touch could put me back. As I glided through the water, frictionless, I neared my immobile body. My face was frozen in fear, eyes shut during the moment I thought would be my last. I held out my hand, casting a thin, yellow glow over my face. What I saw was a woman afraid to let go, but also someone who was so tired of being afraid. I wondered how long I'd looked that way, how many years people looked at me as I did now and wondered where my happiness had gone. I wanted to tell the woman I was then that it would be okay. That there would come a day when I wouldn't have to be afraid anymore. My fingers wiped away a passing piece of kelp that had snagged on my ear. As I touched the skin of my frozen body, I felt the connection like a rising electrical shock, the same sensation I had when I switched myself off in the first place.

I can go back.

In my excitement, I almost forgot that I'd be returning to a body still on the verge of death. I tried to loosen the tape around my hands. My fingers sizzled with electric energy begging me to flip my internal switch, but the tape was just as frozen as my body. I'd have to chance it. No longer anchored in the car's whirlpool, I'd at least have a few seconds to get back up to the surface. I didn't hesitate. Reaching for my face once again, I flipped the switch.

I came back into the world and nearly gasped for air. The ocean shocked me back to reality, salty water stinging my eyes. No longer floating in my ethereal form, I was once again bound and sinking. I could only move my legs like a paddle, back and forth, but I pushed them as hard as my fatigued body would allow, thrashing with my arms to lift myself higher. Every second brought me closer to survival. My chest ached to fill with air again. At last, I crashed through the surface, stars shining bright overhead, and barked through a series of hoarse breaths. I struggled to right myself so I could float on my back. Once there, I took enough breaths to calm myself.

The shore was close enough for me to float in on the waves. I reached the rocky sand on my hands and knees, sliding across the beach like a mermaid. I shimmied over to a piece of rock sticking up out of the sand and raked the tape on my hands across its edge until I could tear it apart. My hands finally free, I unraveled my legs and feet next. I collapsed with my back on the sand and let my eyes drift across the stars above. For a moment, everything seemed to stand still. I smiled at the irony. A thin cloud slid over the moon. I closed my eyes and enjoyed the calm of the ocean lapping at the shore.

Resting under the stars, tasting the sweetness of the air, I felt whole again. I was still a part of this world.

Still alive.

It was incredible just how much of a weight had been lifted off my shoulders, knowing that Britt couldn't chase me anymore. She was gone. Truly gone. I'd always worried that if

I did manage to get rid of her one day, I'd secretly feel a sense of loss, despite everything she'd done. But that was just an echo of her abuse. She would want me to pine for her, to question whether I could survive without her. I'd answered that question while watching her car disappear into the abyss.

My work wasn't over, though. There was still another monster to see off into the depths before I could rest. I sat up —tired and bruised—and tried to brace myself for one last task—stopping Gemma.

CHAPTER NINETEEN

I MADE it back to the city thanks to a few kind souls willing to give a ride to someone who looked like a drowned rat. I certainly felt like one. Along the way, I spent my time piecing together what I meant to do when I faced Gemma again. No matter how many scenarios I pictured, the same solution kept bubbling up over and over—I knew I would need to figure out a way to keep her away from Amaryn. Chaos wouldn't let me freeze Gemma, but I could freeze my body while I held her. She wouldn't just let me walk up and give her a nice squeeze while I waited for the WU to show up, though. I needed a distraction.

At least for that, I had an idea that might work. I eventually made it back to my rental car and took a trip back through Snoqualmie Pass to gather what I needed. Or rather, who.

Cedric bobbed along in the passenger seat like a crash test dummy. I dressed him in a black rain poncho I'd found at the gas station on the road to the lake house. Combined with his red eyes and unruly hair, it made him look like a black widow spider. We cruised along the empty streets of early morning back to Seattle and the Valhalla Tower.

As I expected, the city center was on lockdown after Gemma's storm. Overhead, a red cloud continued to swirl around the top of the tower. The Chaos rain had stopped, but the storm's threat still hung there like a promise. Set against the rising sun, it was a shining beacon of Gemma's power for all of Seattle to see. I remembered being intimidated the first time I saw the tower. Now here I was again, full of inexplicable power, yet still harboring some the same doubts.

The closest we could get was a parking lot two blocks away from the building. I lifted Cedric from my car and carried him in my arms. He was as light as a child, his body emaciated while he'd been jumping from one Chaos-ridden universe to another. Back at the lake house, I'd walked through his bookstore to find him in one of those worlds. He was all too eager to hear my ideas on thwarting Gemma. I promised I would come back and tell him the whole story when it was over, but I needed a favor first. It was that favor I hoped he was fulfilling while we walked.

As we neared Valhalla, we ran into a barricade of fences and yellow tape cordoning off the area. A World Union security guard stopped us when we got too close.

Saves me a phone call, I guess.

"Authorized personnel only," he said.

I caught a glimpse of two containment cells being loaded into the back of a military truck. Samuel, the man who tried to absorb me into the void of his skin, pounded his star-filled fists against the glass while he waited to be put in the back. I could just make out the body-stealing little girl inside the other cell. They were wo people whose lives were already irreparably harmed by Gemma's madness.

Another man, older than the guard and with enough colorful ribbons on his lapels to mark him as someone in charge, overheard us and came to stand at the barricade. "I'm the regional commander. You must be Zoe Daniel."

I hesitated. "You know me?"

"I wasn't sure if we'd find you in that tower along with those two in the truck. A friend of mine has been trying to get in touch with you for a very long time." He seemed to measure me up with a look. "We're aware of what Gemma Weeks has done. What do you and your friend here intend to do about it?"

"I'm not trying to kill her," I answered, "but I have an idea how to stop her."

At least I hoped I did. I filled him in on what my intentions were—to freeze myself and Gemma so they could subdue her peacefully. He turned back to the other officer and motioned toward the collection of WU vehicles nearby. The officer jogged off. Once we were alone, the commander pulled back the barricade to let us through.

"We can go in?" I asked.

"We're coming with you."

"You can't," I said. The thought of what Gemma would do to anyone caught in between us made my stomach churn. "Please. It's too dangerous. If she sees anyone else, she'll panic. Let me handle it."

He craned his neck to look up.

"Fifteen minutes," I said. "That's all I need." I wasn't sure if my plan would work, but I knew it would be quick if it did.

"You have ten," the man replied. "And only because you've been vouched for by my colleagues. But if I see so much as a drop of red coming from the sky again, we're bringing Gemma Weeks out of there, one way or another."

It was enough of a head start. I said a silent thank you to whomever thought so highly of me at the WU.

We left the blockade behind us and started for the tower. The sidewalks outside Valhalla still held the stain of Chaos. I left footprints in the viscous red puddles outside the building. I pushed my way through the revolving front door. Inside, the lobby was a ghost town and as still as the Silence. I grabbed one of the courtesy wheelchairs parked near the main entrance and lowered Cedric into it.

To my surprise, my palm scan worked on the elevator. I had no delusions about surprising Gemma, but this was a clear sign that she was expecting me. We rode the elevator to the fortieth floor. I couldn't help the feeling of speeding toward the edge of a cliff again, only this time I was the one driving instead of Britt. Cedric and I stepped out into the reception area when the doors parted. An eerie stillness greeted us. The lights were still off as we wove our way past empty cubicles. Through the lab's entry, the door to Gemma's office stood open, a small shaft of yellow light reaching out into the hallway.

I walked inside, oddly flush with confidence in what I was about to do. The sensation of trusting myself felt faintly familiar, like a language I'd forgotten I knew. The inside of her office still had the facade of her old home. Gemma stood facing a wooden dormer, her hands clasped behind her back as she stared down at the streets dyed blood red. Amaryn laid beside her. Her quickly decaying body sat inside of a clawfoot tub filled with Chaos—moving and alive as it slithered around her. A sheen of red coated the loose, shriveled skin of Amaryn's arms and chest. Her hair was slick with it.

"I should've known that woman would fail," Gemma said. "Always remember, Zoe. You can never trust anyone but yourself."

She turned to face me. When she did, there was a rare unguarded moment of genuine surprise—the first time she'd ever shown it. I pushed the wheelchair closer, stopping far enough away so that she wouldn't be worried about me reaching her in one trip to the Silence. I didn't want to spook her into doing something even more drastic than what she'd already done. It took all I had to maintain my appearance of calm beneath her penetrating stare. My chest vibrated with pounding heartbeats.

"You've brought a friend," she said, trying to regain her composure. Still, she couldn't completely cover the simmering look she gave Cedric. "If you think this husk scares me, you're sadly mistaken, Zoe. It's a little late for blackmail."

"I didn't bring him here to scare you."

"Then why is this madman in my house?"

She was already starting to think of this place as her home, this office playing pretend. I reminded myself that the clock was ticking, and the WU wouldn't stay away for long. I needed to make my move. "I brought him here because he knows someone who can help Amaryn."

She looked at Cedric again, this time with greedy eyes. "Who?"

"I want your promise first," I said. "Promise me that you'll call off the storm. No one else gets infected."

"If this mystery friend of yours exists—if they can cure Amaryn—you have my word," she said quickly.

"That means Chaos goes away, Gemma. All of it."

"You want me to give up the one bargaining chip I have against those wolves outside? No. Never. I've given you my concession, now bring me whoever this person is."

She spoke greedily, but it was also clear she meant to budge no further. I looked down at Cedric and flexed my muscle.

In the Silence, the door to his bookshop appeared behind his wheelchair. I stepped through, and this time I found him leaning against a tree in a park filled with art sculptures but bereft of grass and trees. A woman stood beside him, arms crossed, a tall and polished figure next to Cedric's t-shirt and shorts. She was achingly familiar, while not quite fitting into the mental mold I'd fashioned of her. Just seeing her made it seem real, like things were going to be okay after all.

"You think this is going to work?" I asked him.

"Your guess is as good as mine," he said with a shrug. "None of the other Zoes have tried it. Godspeed!"

The woman gingerly made her way toward me. She took my outstretched hand.

"Ready?" I asked her.

"Ready," Amaryn said.

I was terrified that my plan to bring Amaryn back as my distraction would fall apart as soon as she followed me through the door, but just as I had hoped, she came through to the Silence with me, frozen in place along with Gemma in my paused moment in time. I immediately felt the tug of my muscle struggling to hold my flex, so I let go. Amaryn's hand came to life in mine once again.

Gemma didn't react at first. She measured Amaryn—my Amaryn—like a lioness trying to decide if a newborn cub was hers. Then her eyes softened. She held out a hand like she wanted to touch her to see if she was real, then took it back. "Amaryn," she said, her voice threatening to break. "Is that you?"

Amaryn looked at me first. I nodded for her to go ahead.

"It's me," she said.

"I can't believe it." Gemma smiled, releasing one of the tears she was trying so hard to hold back. "You are gorgeous, just like my little girl."

Amaryn glanced around the room until her eyes caught her counterpart in the clawfoot tub by the window, still soaking in a bath of Chaos. She lowered her head.

Gemma moved to the edge of the tub. She spoke quickly, as if she wanted to explain things before my Amaryn was scared away. "She's been ill for some time. I've done all I can to save her."

Amaryn moved closer to the tub. I left Cedric alone in the living room and carefully stepped toward Gemma, prepared to make my move and grab hold of her when I could. Gemma barely acknowledged that I was in the room anymore, still keeping close to the tub but never letting her eyes stray from this other version of her daughter.

"This could've been me," my Amaryn said absently. She brushed her hand along the edge of the tub but stopped short of touching the version of herself in the Chaos.

"You were sick, too?" Gemma asked.

Amaryn nodded.

"But you were cured. Was it Chaos? Did I find someone that helped you?"

"You did. It was Zoe."

Now Gemma looked back over her shoulder to me. Gone was the contempt she'd held in her eyes. It was the look of someone who'd found a use for the tool they meant to throw in the trash. Her tone immediately brightened. "Zoe cured you?"

"My version of her did, yes."

"Where is she?" She turned to address me. "Why didn't you bring her first?"

"I can only bring through one person at a time. I didn't think you'd trust me unless you saw Amaryn for yourself."

"Bring the other Zoe here," Gemma said. "*Now*. There isn't much time."

"We can," I answered. "But you need to do your part first."

"I want to see her," Gemma demanded. "I'm not doing anything until the other version is here."

"This isn't a negotiation. If you want Amaryn back, you'll stop the storm. Now."

Gemma looked ready to bend down and tell her Amaryn to light the world on fire to spite me, but then the smoldering in her eyes eased. She knelt beside the tub. When she leaned forward to whisper commands into her Amaryn's lifeless ear, the air in the room warbled with resonance as her words took hold. I looked out the window behind me. The red cloud circling overhead began to shrink. Gradually, the sky lightened until there was no longer a red hue to the world.

"It's done," Gemma said, standing. "Now do what you've promised."

Amaryn glanced toward me before speaking. She looked so worried. I wanted to tell her that we were almost there, that we were so close to making sure Gemma never hurt anyone again. All we had to do was keep our nerve.

"What's the matter?" Gemma said, looking between us.

"Nothing," Amaryn replied, too quickly. "I should get back so Zoe can help."

Gemma paused, once again taking in the two of us. I didn't like the shift in her eyes, narrowing in focus like she'd finally worked out an optical illusion. "Before you go," she said. "Will I need anything to help my Amaryn? Any medical or lab equipment? I can have it here in a whisper."

"I don't think so. Does she?" Amaryn asked me.

I shook my head. *Just relax. We're almost there.* I took a step closer to Gemma. I was so close to being in place to grab her. Grab her, freeze myself, and then wait as Amaryn got the WU to sedate her so we could stop her for good.

"Nothing?" Gemma sounded incredulous. "How was she able to save you?"

"Oh, I don't know. She didn't really tell me too much about how she did it."

Gemma smiled at us both. I had hoped Amaryn could keep her focus, but Gemma's eyes were on me. She beamed as if she'd just solved a mystery. "Amazing," she said, focusing once again on Amaryn. "Even across other worlds, I can spot your lies."

Amaryn looked at me, panicked.

"There is no Zoe in that world, is there?" Gemma demanded.

"There is! She's…"

"She's dead." It wasn't a question. Gemma seemed to read it on her otherworld daughter 's face.

Amaryn slowly nodded. Anger started to surface behind

her eyes. "You killed so many just to bring me back. All that suffering just so you could have what you wanted. I won't let you do it to anyone else."

Gemma was her old self again. No longer off-balance, she stepped with conviction until she only had to lean forward to whisper in her Amaryn's ear.

"I want to thank you," she said. "You've shown me I was right—that I can use Chaos to find a cure for my little girl. I'm going to bring the storm back, more powerful than before."

"She's dead," Amaryn said. "You know that."

"*She isn't!* Not really. Chaos is infinite. Infinite possibilities. Infinite avenues to get what I'm owed. All I have to do is find the one—the one person who can bring her back to me, just like she was before. Just like you've become."

Gemma knelt beside the tub again. She hadn't whispered a word in her daughter's ear, and I could already feel the air in the room change. No more waiting for the perfect moment. I slipped into the Silence to move closer to the tub so I could freeze her Amaryn before any whispered order could be issued, then I would grab Gemma.

The Chaos encased Amaryn, still writhing and angry in my stationary moment. Gemma's pulsating red form hovered next to her. I reached my hand out for Amaryn's limp arm, but the familiar rush of cold wasn't there as I touched her skin. I didn't understand. I tried another spot to no avail. My mind searched frantically for a reason. Then, as I was losing my hold, I noticed again the sheen of red covering her skin. She was drenched in it. Chaos wouldn't let itself be frozen.

I came out of my flex and fell to my knees next to Gemma's Amaryn. The stench from her body filled my nose. Before I knew it, a blazing rush of pain sprouted from the side of my head as Gemma slammed me against the lip of the tub. I fell to the floor, teetering on the edge of consciousness.

I heard the living Amaryn cry out. The shrillness of her pleading pulled me back some.

"Don't do this!" Amaryn yelled. "Please!"

"What would you have me do? Let her go?"

I tried to stand and couldn't. I could only look up, seeing Amaryn looking back down at me with panicked eyes. Then, something in them changed. For a moment, even through the fog damping my ability to think, I saw something in her that I'd seen so many times in Gemma. It was a look that said she knew exactly what to do and to get out of her way.

"You're going to hurt too many people," she said.

"Not hurt them—Enhance them. Make them better. Make them *capable!*"

"And kill how many?"

Gemma leaned forward to whisper without answering. The air started to warble. I was too groggy to hold a flex, let alone come up with a way to stop her.

"Mother!"

Gemma paused. She looked back at Amaryn, who knelt at her side.

"If you do this, I can't stay here."

"Then go," Gemma said, but the words lacked her usual force.

"My mom—you—she's gone in my world. I never got to say goodbye. If I have to go now, let me say goodbye. Give me that, at least. Please."

Gemma looked back to make sure I was still down. Satisfied that I wasn't a threat, she turned to Amaryn. She tentatively opened her arms as if she was scared of what might happen if she did but more scared to lose her chance.

Amaryn leaned in. They held each other, gingerly at first, but then each of their arms clutched the other like they never wanted to let go.

Amaryn glanced down to me.

I saw now what she wanted. Her arm was close. My head was swimming, and I didn't know how long I could keep the hold, but I slipped into the Silence once more. Amaryn's hand was within reach, holding the writhing red figure of Gemma in her arms. I touched Amaryn's skin. The rush of cold nearly made me scream. I had to let go after flipping my mental switch, but it was done.

When I came back, Gemma was still in her daughter's arms.

"Goodbye," she said.

Amaryn's face was frozen, her eyes squeezed shut. Her arms still firmly clutched Gemma in a tight embrace.

Gemma tried to move. There was nowhere for her to go. "Amaryn?"

With my head still pounding and a shrill ring still filling my ears, I struggled to stand, forcing my body to move to her side.

Gemma's eyes sparked in anger at the sight of me. She leaned her head toward my Amaryn to whisper a command into her ear, but the air never changed. Her words died in a murmur. She might as well have been whispering to a wall.

"What did you do?" she said, glaring up at me. "What did you *do*?" She tried once more to free herself but there was no getting out of Amaryn's stone grasp. She was trapped.

Gemma's eyes turned toward the tub. Resigned to defeat, she closed them just as she started to cry, no longer fighting her daughter's embrace. She held Amaryn tightly.

Gemma didn't say another word.

Footsteps thundered down the hall outside the office. The WU Security team, led by the commander, marched into the room, neural guns raised.

"It's all right," I said, putting myself in between their sights and Gemma. "She can't hurt anyone else."

Amaryn—my Amaryn—still held Gemma in her frozen vice. Cedric sat in his wheelchair, an absent observer. I pictured him anxiously waiting for news on what had gone down. I'd tell him once I guided Amaryn back to her world, but there was something I needed to do first.

My head still pounding, I gingerly pulled Gemma's

Amaryn out of the tub, wrapping her in a blanket from the couch. I covered her face last, silently assuring her—*you can rest now*.

I motioned for the guards to come in. The one in front carried a syringe filled with a sedative, just like I'd asked them to bring. Gemma didn't struggle as the needle went in, but as I walked past her with her daughter in my arms, some life returned to her eyes. It was a look that posed the question she was too proud to ask.

"Don't worry," I told her. "I'll take good care of her."

CHAPTER TWENTY

A GENTLE RAIN followed me over the mountains until I emerged on the other side of the Cascades for the second time that day. A hazy blanket of sunshine welcomed me into the valley. The last few items from my apartment jostled in boxes in the back, while a bouquet of flowers rode in the passenger seat—a last-minute purchase from the store. I took the now-familiar back roads until I got to the lake house driveway and immediately took note of the grass starting to grow tall around the edges of the fence. One more item for the to-do list.

I pulled the car into the open barn doors and grabbed the bundle of flowers from the front seat. The RV I'd rented sat on the edge of the property near the tree line at the base of the mountain. It wasn't much—a small silver pill with a pull-out canopy—but it was a welcome change of pace from the city. Plus, it had a built-in ramp up to the door, which came in handy for when my new roommate needed to get some air.

"Kinda stuffy in here," I said as I unlocked the door. I released the locks on Cedric's wheelchair. "Ready for a change of scenery?"

Flowers tucked into my arm, I backed Cedric out of the RV and pushed him along toward the edge of the lake, past the remnants of the old house, now just a black circle of charred wood. When I returned my Amaryn to her world, Cedric was like a child on Winter's Day as he scribbled notes about Gemma's fate in his book. I asked him one last time if he wanted to come back with me, but he just laughed and said I'd have to settle for carting around his ugly stunt double.

I wore a ponytail draped over my shoulder to keep it tamed against the wind. It felt good to style it that way again. The air near the lake was already starting to get colder as evening approached. It had been so long since I'd been through a change of seasons after years in La Grange, I almost didn't recognize the first notes of fall. Cedric's wheelchair bounced and bucked along the small foot path. I made another mental note to look into getting something with bigger wheels for our little walks.

We came to a stop just before the gravestone. I set the locks on Cedric's chair and adjusted the hat and sunglasses I'd bought for him. You could just barely see the red in his eyes through the lenses.

Finally, I took the flowers and walked them over to the small stone slab that marked Amaryn's grave. I took the old ones away and replaced them with the new—an arrangement of sunflowers and wild Cascade daisies. It felt like a yellow kind of day.

"Things are coming along," I told her. "I'll sign off on the paperwork to take over the property here next Tuesday. Valhalla didn't exactly argue when I asked for this as my severance. Well, this and enough money to keep some food on our picnic table until I can afford to rebuild."

I sat facing the lake, watching with her as the waves lapped against the shore.

"No one's telling me what they did with the Chaos, which means the WU probably has it buried in a warehouse somewhere. They asked me for advice on how to handle it. I told them they'd be better off shooting it into the sun. I wasn't kidding.

"On that subject, your mom still isn't talking to anyone about it—or anything else. From what I've read, they're keeping her behind two panes of glass just to be safe." I thought back to the pictures I saw of Gemma and Amaryn in the lake house hallway before it burned down, the last of the Weeks family matriarchs. Gemma's end was her own doing, but for all her faults, she loved her daughter to the last. "Maybe when things die down a bit, I can convince someone to let her come see you."

A gust of wind swept across the grass bordering the rectangle of river stones covering Amaryn. I stood and readjusted the sunflowers on her gravestone.

Behind us, car tires rumbled slowly over the crushed rock driveway. A nondescript gray sedan wound along the path. I hadn't expected visitors so soon, but by the generic looks of the car, the World Union wasn't done with me yet. I stood by Cedric's chair and waited for them to make it down.

After a few nervous twists and turns around the potholes, the car came to a stop beside the barn. I expected it to be the squad commander again from the WU Security team, but instead, a woman stepped out with a brown shoulder bag slung across her sweater. Long brown hair blew across her face. She kept trying to push it out of the way of her smile while she walked through the grass.

"Hello!" she said when she got close. "You're Zoe, right? Please tell me you're Zoe and that I haven't just flown across the continent to embarrass myself."

"I'm Zoe all right."

"Oh, thank gods." She came to a stop in front of Cedric and waved to him.

I picked up his limp arm and waved back.

"Oh. Okay. Uh, well, hello again! My name's Emmy

Saria." She couldn't help looking down at Cedric. "He's not dead, right?"

I shook my head. "Just off in his own little world."

"I see. I think. Anyway, it's so good to finally meet you."

Dr. Emmy Saria. I knew the name, although of all the people I expected at my doorstep after the business with Valhalla, she was pretty far down the list. Still, I wasn't unprepared.

"You're heading up the PRISM project for the WU," I said. "You were the first researcher to work with the alien woman that landed a couple years ago, and if I'm not mistaken, you're working closely with Commander Rector's team now."

"Impressive! You've done your homework."

I smiled. "What can I do for you, Dr. Saria?" I braced for a sales pitch. Knowing who she was—and who she worked with—I could only assume they wanted to offer me a job to keep me under close watch.

"For a start, can I live with you? This place is gorgeous." She beamed as she took in the mountains.

"The camper's a little crowded, unfortunately, but I know an apartment for rent in Seattle if you're interested."

"I wish," she replied. "Alas, the commander does expect me back at work next week. Speaking of work…"

I held up my hand. "I'm not interested."

"But—"

"Listen," I said. "Dr. Saria, it's an honor to meet you—really. You're basically the most famous person I've ever talked to."

She laughed quickly and feigned embarrassment.

"But I'm not looking for a job with the WU right now. I'm sorry."

"I see," she said. "Well, if I had come here to offer you a job, I'd be very disappointed."

She swatted at a bee circling her head. From everything

I'd heard about the WU, they didn't like taking no for an answer. I entered the Silence and froze the bee in place, coming back out of my moment to stand on the other side of Cedric. It was showboating, for sure, but I wanted to make sure she was off-balance if she was about to attempt a strong-arm recruitment.

Emmy did a slight double-take when she saw me on the opposite side of the wheelchair. She looked at the bee, now motionless, and touched its wings. "So cool."

"You were saying?"

"Oh! Right." She took a step away from the bee so it wasn't right between us. "I'm not here to offer you a job, Zoe. I mean, you're super impressive as a researcher, don't get me wrong. I'd hire you in a minute to work in my labs. But we wanted to offer you something better."

"And what would that be?"

"A chance to make a difference." She paused and then huffed while she reached into her bag. "Gods, that sounded so corny. Look, all I'm trying to say is that the WU wanted you for a job. I came here to see what *you* wanted to do. Whatever that is—I want to help." She took a handheld tablet out of her bag and handed it to me. "And I have a stupid amount of money in my budget to do just that."

I didn't doubt that the World Union had money, but what gave me pause was that she asked me what I wanted to do. I couldn't remember the last time someone had asked me that.

The tablet showed a list of folders on the screen, each labeled with someone's name. I scanned the list, not sure what I was looking at, until I saw Samuel's name near the bottom.

"Is this a list of people infected with Chaos?" I asked.

She nodded. "Partial list, anyway. These are the people we know about that have exhibited abilities."

There were so many. I thumbed through two pages. "What do you want me to do?"

"I was sort of hoping you could tell me."

I took a look at the list again. I thought back to my first few days struggling with what Chaos had done to me and imagined what I needed at that time. "They're probably feeling isolated and afraid. Their entire world has been upended. I'd want to help them make sense of it all."

"I thought you might say that," she said with a smile. "It's all settled, then. Consider yourself the first recipient of the Dr. Emmy Saria Chaos Grant—cooler name to be determined later."

After Gemma, I was all too wary of job offers that seemed too good to be true. "What are you expecting in return?"

"Solid question. I won't lie—Rector wanted you in Triton where he could keep an eye on you—but I convinced him that if I was going to head up Research, then he needed to let me do my job how I wanted to do it. He's not the kind of boss who takes no with a smile, you know what I mean? But he agreed. And just like I want to run my projects how I see fit, I want to give you the same freedom to run yours."

I had so many ideas already. There was one thing at the top of my list though. "I want to build a place for them. Here. They'll need somewhere they can feel safe."

Emmy looked around again. The landscape seemed to want to show off, with the Cascades suddenly awash in light as the sun came out from behind a cloud. "Perfect," she said.

Before she walked back to her car, Emmy gave me her number, and we made plans to meet up again to go over specifics the next morning. She jokingly asked if I wanted to meet her celebrity partner in crime while she was here. I half wondered if I'd just signed up to meet all those friends Cedric told me about.

Cedric and I watched as she drove through the gate, leaving us alone with Amaryn once more.

I looked back at the burnt remains of Gemma's house and imagined what could be. What *would* be.

There was a lot to plan for now. The people on the tablet

were going to need help. I looked around at the tips of the Cascades and took in a deep breath of cool air. Gemma had once brought me here under a false promise of protection. Now I meant to make that promise a reality for others.

I brushed the dirt from my jeans before saying goodnight to Amaryn. Cedric watched the coming sunset through his unblinking stare.

"Come on," I said as I turned his chair back toward the trailer. "Let's get you home."

Acknowledgments

Hey. It's been a minute.

Honestly, I've been waiting for me to write the next book, too. I released ATALANTA during the early months of the pandemic. Then, as it did for everyone else in the world, life got real weird, real fast. No amount of "I want to write the next story" could overcome the desire to sit in the house and play games to avoid thinking about how awful the world was. My bread and butter is creating modern versions of mythology, and mythology is largely a reflection of our world. I was in no mood to look in the mirror back then.

Once things started to get somewhat back to normal, I slowly got back into working on WRAITH. I found a new critique group of writers, and their support has been invaluable. I'll get to those beauties later. I eventually struggled through a first draft, then another, and then about a billion others until I felt like I got the story I wanted on the page. What's left is exactly what I hoped Zoe's story would be when I first drew up an outline in 2020. She's going to be a *force* in the future. I can't wait until she gets to meet the rest of the crew.

Speaking of—I haven't forgotten about Prism and Atty. Prism is probably hanging on a porch, drinking wine with Winnie in between missions right now, while Atty is somewhere in L.A., most likely spending her free time building her own private army. There's one more book to go before I throw everyone together (probably with disastrous results). Next up is GORGON, and I'm saving what I hope is the best for last. While I kind of just dipped my toe into horror with Zoe's book, Viv's story is definitely one for spooky season. It's also going to see the return of a character from Prism's finale, and this time he is *not* playing around.

Anyway, let's get to some thank yous.

First of all, I couldn't do any of this without the support of my wife, our kiddos, and the rest of my family. I'm so lucky I get to be a character in your life stories. I love you all.

A huge thank you also goes out to my critique group of writers. Ru, Liz, Laura, Kendra, Pat, and David—you're all fantastic writers, incredible friends, and all-around good humans. A day will come when they're all famous, and I'm totally going to re-release these acknowledgements to include their last names so I can ride their coattails.

While they only know me from putting "Matt" on coffee cups, big thank yous go to the good people at Cafe Diem and La Vita Dolce. I needed to get back to writing in comfy coffee shops once things got back to normal, and they're two of the comfiest and coffee-est around.

Finally, a huge, huge thank you to everyone at BDA Publishing. They're the ones responsible for putting Zoe's story in your hands. Mel, Jana, Katie, and the rest: I'm so happy to be a part of what you're doing. Thank you for believing in this world of stories I'm trying to build.

That's it, friendos. Take care of yourselves out there. I'll see you next time—unless you find me in one of those comfy coffee shops first.

About the Author

Hi. I'm Matt.

Mythology is high on my revolving list of hyperfixations. I've taken my love of Greek myths and mixed those characters with modern stories of people learning to cope with superhuman abilities. Everything I write takes place in the same universe because I like to think my characters would try to get together for game nights.

My NC roots run deep and I currently live in the Triangle area with my wife, kiddos, and two ridiculous dogs. While I'm a practiced hermit, you can usually tempt me out of the house with a cozy coffee shop or tickets to a soccer game.

When I'm not writing or buying things based solely on its sweet, sweet artwork, I can usually be found in an airport terminal because I won't rest until I've bought Magic cards in every major city.

Also By Matt King

The Circle War

Godsend

The Last Winter

Ascension

The New Mythology

Prism

Atalanta

Wraith

Short Stories

A Monster In The Maze

The Tria

The First Death Of August